SHOWCASE

A CHARLOTTE SAMS MYSTERY

ALISON GLEN

SIMON & SCHUSTER

NEW YORK   LONDON   TORONTO   SYDNEY   TOKYO   SINGAPORE

SIMON & SCHUSTER
SIMON & SCHUSTER BUILDING
ROCKEFELLER CENTER
1230 AVENUE OF THE AMERICAS
NEW YORK, NEW YORK 10020

DESIGNED BY SONGHEE KIM
MANUFACTURED IN THE UNITED STATES OF AMERICA

1   3   5   7   9   10   8   6   4   2

LIBRARY OF CONGRESS CATALOGING-IN-PUBLICATION DATA
Glen, Alison.
    Showcase: a Charlotte Sams mystery/by Alison Glen.
        p.   cm.
    I. Title.
    PS3557.L4418S48   1992
    813'.54—dc20   92–16941
                                                          CIP
ISBN: 978-1-4767-9995-7

NOTE

The Son of Heaven exhibition, which figures prominently in this book, was real and did show in Seattle and Columbus during 1988 and 1989. The "nine five-claw dragon rule" and the *National Geographic* article mentioned are also real. However, the incidents in the book are entirely fictional, as are all the main characters. The Columbus landmarks mentioned exist, but most of the companies and the Institute for Research on Career Development do not. Of the people mentioned in the book, only Governor Richard Celeste, Dagmar Celeste, Mayor Dana Rinehart, Heisman Trophy winner Howard "Hopalong" Cassady, and jazz singer Diane Schuur are not the work of the author's imagination.

For assistance in bringing *Showcase* to print, the following people are thanked: Vernon Broberg, Carolyn Burton, Harry Burton, Thomas Chapman, Kathleen Cook, Clarine Cotton, Edward Dunbar, John Hogan, Maeve Ennis, Susan Imel, Susanne Jaffe, Christopher James, Suzanne James, Sandra Kerka, Paula Kurth, Bill Lowry, Cynthia Macaluso, Glenna Meredith, Jan Meredith, Audrey Snedecor, Maria Therres, Naomi Therres, and Judith Wagner.

For support for the notion that mysteries can and should be written by women, special thanks go to the members of Sisters in Crime and Malice Domestic.

PROLOGUE

November 23

An item in the local section of the *Seattle Times* might have excited more comment if it had not appeared the day before Thanksgiving.

Guard Found Dead

Security guard Irvin T. Jackson, 48, of 291 Brendan Ct., was pronounced dead this morning at the "Son of Heaven" Chinese art exhibit. Police said Jackson's body was discovered by day-shift guards at the 6 A.M. shift change. The body was found slumped over the panel that controls the exhibit's security system. Police are continuing their investigation, but their initial findings revealed no signs of violence or a break-in. Nothing from the exhibit was missing, according to exhibit officials. The exhibit of imperial Chinese art works will occupy Flag Center through January.

November 30

The following paragraph in the weekly police news column brought the incident to a close.

PROLOGUE

Autopsy Complete

The autopsy of Irvin T. Jackson, the security guard found dead at the "Son of Heaven" art exhibit last Wednesday, today confirmed that he died of a heart attack. Medical records indicate the 48-year-old Jackson had been treated for angina. He lived at 291 Brendan Ct. Police have completed their investigation of the incident.

On the front page, a feature story described the upcoming visit of Dr. Chen Ching, a Chinese art scholar who was to spend December with the Son of Heaven exhibit. Ching was scheduled to present two lectures that exhibit officials hoped would boost sagging attendance at the show. Upon completing its run on January 20 at Flag Center, the site of the 1962 Seattle World's Fair, the Son of Heaven exhibit was expected to open at the end of February in Columbus, Ohio.

C Sunday Evening, February 26

harlotte Sams looked out her bedroom window at the pouring rain, trying to figure out how to arrive at the Son of Heaven gala without looking as if she'd gone through a car wash. Ordinarily, she was not one to fuss about getting a little damp. But having to trek through a deluge in dressy attire could take all the fun out of going to the party.

So far there had been little sign of fun. To begin with, Charlotte had been coerced into attending the gala by her friend Lou Toreson, who would be serving as a volunteer guide for student tours at the Son of Heaven exhibit for the duration of the school year. Lou's interests had a way of involving entirely innocent bystanders, and Charlotte had the feeling she was going to learn a lot more about Chinese art during the next few months than she had ever wanted to. Fortunately, Lou had wrangled their two three-hundred-fifty-dollar tickets to tonight's affair at no cost to Charlotte. Lou had offered to try to find a third ticket for Charlotte's husband Walt, but he had declined the offer, saying he would be content to see the exhibit with what he considered "regular" folks after it opened to the public the following day.

Charlotte had considered backing out herself an hour earlier. Right before she started dressing for the evening's festivities, her cousin Melanie Stevenson had phoned. Me-

lanie just wanted to say how glad she was to learn that
Charlotte would be sharing a table tonight with her and her
art history professor husband Phil, whom Charlotte loathed.
It promised to be a night to remember.

Charlotte stepped away from the window and caught her
reflection in a wall mirror. Despite her mood, she was
pleased with the image she saw. Her short dark-blond hair
was swept back rather elegantly from her squarish face,
which looked considerably younger than her forty years.
She wore a forest-green velvet chemise with silk trim at the
neckline and wrists. Her new high heels were a dark-gold
color. For jewelry, the only piece even vaguely Chinese was
an antique brooch that she wore not as a pin but on a flat
gold chain. The oval brooch was pale-green carved jade and
had been a gift from Walt to celebrate the birth of their son
Tyler almost twelve years earlier.

Tyler and his friend Kevin were lying on the living room
floor watching a Nickelodeon commercial for an upcoming
sitcom. Charlotte considered the Nick promos to be much
more creative than the shows they advertised. She paused
to watch a serious-voiced announcer tell young viewers that
three out of eight adult men eventually resemble crotchety
old Mr. Wilson on the "Dennis the Menace Show." The
announcer advised them to watch out for signs of incipient
crotchetiness in their neighbors, even in their own fathers.

"Speaking of fathers, Ty," she said, "if yours doesn't get
back from the construction site in about five minutes, I'm
going to have to leave anyway."

"Whatever," was Tyler's reply, his eyes still on the screen.

"I'm sure he won't be long," Charlotte continued. "The
rain probably slowed down traffic."

"You look nice, Mrs. Sams," Kevin said, smiling. Tyler
rolled his eyes at his friend. Undeterred, Kevin said, "I don't
see you this dressed up very often."

"*Nobody* sees me this dressed up very often," she said.
"Thanks."

She put on a heavy wool cape to protect her dress, told

the boys good-bye, and was standing on her wide front porch, ready to leave, when Walt hurried up the steps.

"Hi," he said, and kissed her lightly. "Sorry I took so long. The traffic was just creeping along out east."

He had returned from checking a construction site where some of his company's equipment was being leased. He often made such checks, even during the weekend, since he felt his customers rarely took adequate security precautions to protect the lift equipment they rented from him. He frequently complained that construction foremen gave about as much thought to ordering a piece of his five-ton equipment as they did when ordering pizza and that, once the equipment arrived, they paid as much attention to it as they did empty pizza boxes.

"You look nice, by the way."

"Thanks. You're the second fellow to compliment me this evening, and the first was not our son," Charlotte said, smiling. "Ty and Kevin are watching TV. There's chili in the refrigerator and a new *Games* magazine on the hall table."

Walt nodded, pleased by the prospect of a relaxing evening doing crosswords and cryptoquotes. "Enjoy yourself," he said.

Hunching her shoulders under the cape, Charlotte ran to her car at the curb.

The rain continued heavily as she threaded her five-year-old red LeBaron convertible through the narrow streets of Clintonville, one of Columbus's northern neighborhoods. Like many of the city's residents, those who lived in Charlotte's neighborhood tended to be white-collar workers employed at the area's several universities, research institutes, state government offices, and insurance company home offices.

The houses she passed were nearly all two stories tall but were otherwise an eclectic mix of clapboard, brick, and stone. Wooded ravines wound through some of the neighborhood, giving it a rustic atmosphere.

Right then the atmosphere seemed merely dreary as

Charlotte left Clintonville, crossed over the Olentangy River and, five minutes later, turned into Lou's neighborhood, where Columbus abuts its wealthy western suburb, Upper Arlington.

Lou's street was named SunnyBrook, as in Rebecca's farm. Its quaintness was underscored by the fact that all the houses on Lou's side of the street backed up to the research-and-demonstration farms owned and operated by Ohio State University. In the midst of a sprawling cityscape Lou could look out her back windows and see open fields, occasionally interrupted by grazing cattle and by plant experiments conducted by OSU's agronomy department.

Lou must have seen Charlotte pull into the driveway, for her front door opened immediately and a short, umbrella-shielded figure hurried toward the car. Once inside, she fluffed her salt-and-pepper hair back into its Dutch Boy cut. She smiled triumphantly at Charlotte and said, "We're off!"

As they drove downtown, the car was about as cozy as convertibles get, with the foggy windows and the steady swipe of the windshield wipers contributing to a pleasant sense of isolation. Lou, who hated to drive, nevertheless gave occasional driving instructions to Charlotte and remained cheerful as Charlotte ignored them.

The two women had been friends for years, since Charlotte had interviewed Lou, a psychologist, for a local magazine article about the research on women's career patterns Lou was conducting at the Institute for Research on Career Development on Ohio State's campus.

Charlotte had been, and still was, a free-lance writer. While Ty was young she had worked out of an office at home, writing her articles on a schedule that permitted her to be home before and after Ty's school day. For the last year, she had enjoyed the luxury of working in a rented office in Clintonville and had even hired a part-time assistant, Claudia Pepperdine, a young woman whose natural curiosity and organizational skills had impressed Charlotte.

Lou had reversed Charlotte's pattern, since she was now

doing consulting out of her home. She had retired from her full-time job the year before, at age fifty, when OSU offered a generous buy-out package.

Now Lou suggested that perhaps Walt had changed his mind and wished she had gotten a ticket to the gala for him after all.

"Hardly," Charlotte replied. "He's recently discovered those puzzles called cryptic crosswords that have weird, seemingly meaningless clues. Have you seen those?"

"Yes."

"Well, yesterday he was going around the house trying to think of a seven-letter word for the clue 'wonderful under the citrus.' I picked up a new puzzle magazine for him when I was at the bookstore this morning, so I'm sure he's in puzzle heaven at this very moment."

"Sublime," said Lou.

"Well, if that's the kind of evening you wanted, why are we trekking downtown to this inflated dinner party?"

"I mean, 'sublime' is a seven-letter word for 'wonderful under the citrus.' "

"Oh," said Charlotte, to whom Walt's and Lou's skill at puzzles and word games was a minor but long-standing annoyance.

She asked again why Lou had insisted they attend the gala.

"It's this consultant lifestyle, Char. When you're not working full time, you have lots more energy—not to mention time—to indulge your various interests, and at the moment, Chinese art is of interest to me."

"I can tell."

"Hobnobbing with the rich and famous isn't, but who knows? It may become an important interest." Lou grinned, revealing a Wife-of-Bath gap between her front teeth. "This may be only the first of many exciting evenings for us, Charlotte."

"I wouldn't count too heavily on my participation, if I were you," Charlotte commented. Nonetheless, she felt her spirits lift, responding to the company of someone who was so obviously ready to have a good time. She eased her grip on the steering wheel and felt her shoulders relax, too. The rain even slacked off some.

She smiled as she said, "When I told Ty that you're going to volunteer at Son of Heaven, he thought you were joining a convent."

Lou chuckled. The show's name stemmed from the fact that all its items had belonged to the Chinese emperors or those close to them, and every emperor had called himself the Son of Heaven.

"We volunteers got a sneak preview of the building yesterday," she said. "They've spent several million dollars fixing it up," she added, referring to Columbus Central, the former downtown high school that had been closed five years before, due to population shifts to the suburbs. Central had been converted to house the exhibit.

Charlotte had never been in Central, having attended high school near Dayton. But, she told Lou, the teenaged Walt had watched basketball games there when his Linden McKinley High School Panthers had played the Central High Pirates.

"He told me to look for a life-size photograph of Hopalong Cassady that was always displayed in Central's entry hallway."

"They had a picture of a cowboy in their school's entry?"

Charlotte smiled. "No, a picture of a football player. He's Central High School's claim to fame. He graduated from there in the early fifties, played football for Ohio State, and won the Heisman Trophy. The life-size photograph, Walt says, shows Hopalong in full football regalia."

"That and twenty-two centuries of Chinese art may be just too much for one night."

"I'm afraid it's Phil Stevenson who will be too much for me," Charlotte said grimly. She told Lou about her cousin Melanie's call and that they had been assigned to the same table.

"So what's so bad about Phil Stevenson?"

"Well, he's one of those people who just instantly rub you the wrong way," Charlotte explained. "I don't know how he can engender such terrible feelings in other people so fast, but he manages."

"Perhaps he has some redeeming social value once one looks beneath the surface?"

"No. Underneath, he's even worse than you thought. He generally acts as though the rest of us are brainless, and he's forever correcting people."

Lou blanched as Charlotte changed lanes between widely spaced cars, but Charlotte didn't notice. "It drives Walt absolutely crazy when Phil corrects him," she said.

"Doesn't he correct you more often than Walt?" Lou asked. "That kind of person usually seems to pick on women more than men."

"Not really."

"Your cousin Melanie doesn't find him objectionable?"

"She must want to clobber him sometimes, but she never lets on. Melanie was *never* very spunky, even when we were kids, but I can't imagine why she puts up with her husband."

"There are lots of objectionable people in the world, Charlotte."

"Sure, but Phil is more consistently objectionable than most of them. He's such an intellectual snob. And he never misses an opportunity to lord it over someone—anyone."

She paused to recall examples of Phil's behavior. "For instance, at the last family reunion we attended, some of the older kids asked Phil to play a game of Trivial Pursuit. Well, instead of declining in a nice way, he just brushed them off by saying that they hadn't *lived* long enough to know any trivia."

"That does seem unnecessarily harsh," Lou said.

"Right. Why would he dismiss them that way? He had managed not only to refuse to play with them but to spoil their game with one another by saying they weren't up to it. Phil, of course, seemed unaware that he had hurt their feelings."

"How sensitive of him."

The double doors at the end of the walkway, also painted red and studded with what looked like the ends of thick brass dowels, were shrouded in a swirling vapor. The ethereal effect was created, Charlotte supposed, by dry ice hidden somewhere along the pavement.

"Something tells me we won't be seeing that life-size portrait of Hopalong Cassady," she whispered to Lou.

Inside the double doors, the guests were greeted by a Chinese child who smiled, bowed, and offered a long-stemmed red rose to each woman. The entry seemed spacious with its sixteen-foot ceilings. However, faint odors of fresh paint and carpet glue still lingered.

Charlotte and Lou checked their wraps in a small classroom off to the side that had been converted for that purpose. Then, Chinese "lion dancers" wearing filmy, brightly colored costumes, led them toward the room in which they would be dining.

That room contained no hints of its previous incarnation as Central High School's gymnasium. At the near end were arranged a head table and the thirty round tables at which guests would be seated in groups of ten. At the far end, at the bottom of a considerable slope and in near darkness, the guests could make out indistinct forms of art and artifacts. And on the walls hung a timeline of Chinese history illustrated with large color photographs of art from each period represented in the show.

The lion dancers led them to one of the round linen-covered tables at which several guests were already seated, including Charlotte's cousin Melanie Stevenson and her husband Phil. Charlotte introduced Lou. Phil barely acknowledged the introduction and, typically, was not all that friendly to Charlotte, either.

Melanie had smiled sweetly at Lou. Charlotte noticed that even on this festive occasion, Melanie was wearing a very conservative dress with a high neckline. However, she had done something complicated with her usually limp brown hair and looked the better for it.

Charlotte craned her neck to read a large wall poster near their table, thinking that if she couldn't see the art, at least she could read about it. The poster read:

Several hundred rulers controlled China during the more than 2,200 years the imperial institution endured. Most are now forgotten. But these works made by anonymous artisans and craftsmen live on. It is no small irony that the Son of Heaven is best seen today through the achievements of men and women of no status and no name.

Nicely put, thought Charlotte.

A tall, slim, middle-aged woman in a flattering Chinese red sheath rose from her seat at the head table and accepted a cordless microphone from the lion dancer who stood slightly behind her chair. With her bright dress and upswept black hair, the woman made a dramatic figure as she spoke into the microphone to welcome the group.

Charlotte recognized the director of the Columbus Museum of Art, Libby Peyton Fox. Libby had headed the museum for about two years and was a rather high-profile director, proving herself adept at getting corporate support for the museum and becoming a media darling by being easily available and eminently quotable. Even now a *Columbus Dispatch* photographer was snapping away as Libby spoke.

"We at the Columbus Museum of Art are delighted to welcome you to our exciting exhibit, Son of Heaven: Imperial Arts of China," Libby said. "We are grateful for the efforts of literally hundreds of people who have worked so hard to bring this show to Columbus and to install it so beautifully in our renovated Columbus Central."

There was a polite round of applause before she went on.

"Let me introduce some of those people."

She quickly named several individuals who played key

E ven with the lights up, some of the art works remained in semidarkness. The items exhibited in this room were those the emperors and those at court wore or used as they fulfilled their public, governmental responsibilities. Hence, the area's designation as the Outer Court.

Among the items displayed were the dragon robes and jewelry the emperors wore on state occasions. However, most guests were immediately drawn to the central exhibit in the area: the lavish throne-room ensemble that contained the eighteenth-century wooden throne intricately carved with dragons and covered with gold lacquer.

Surrounding the throne were tall, narrow pagoda-shaped bronze incense burners; large cloisonné elephants that symbolized world peace; tall, thin bronze cranes whose mouths held candle holders; and fat, squat bronze figures of indeterminate animal visage, called "auspicious beasts."

Among the other displays in the Outer Court were fifteen matte black showcases shaped like humans wearing ankle-length robes. The forms were about seven feet tall and eight inches thick. Their surfaces were of a Formica-like material. In the "chest" and "back" area of each—as though the forms were wearing them—were displayed either a necklace from the Ming dynasty or embroidered rectangles of rank insignia from the Qing dynasty.

The insignia were gorgeous—brilliantly colored rectangles of embroidered silk. The central figure in each was either a colorful bird or an animal on a very busy background. A placard explained that the insignia with birds had been worn by civilian officials. Military men wore the ones with animals.

It was while Charlotte was admiring the insignia that she heard Phil Stevenson's wild laughter.

Staggering slightly in front of the showcase that contained an imperial white jade necklace, he had attracted the attention of several people, but they all looked away, embarrassed. Charlotte, however, approached him. By now his laughter seemed a little forced.

"You hicks!" Phil cried. "Snookered and don't even know it. Where's Libby Fox? Somebody get that bitch over here."

The guests within earshot looked shocked and tried harder to ignore him. He recognized Charlotte and slurred, "Won't talk to you."

But in a moment he started in again. Among his ramblings could be heard "recognize a fake," and that word drew people to him like a magnet. In just a few seconds, Charlotte was joined by several guests whose curiosity had overcome their embarrassment at the scene Phil was creating. He was surrounded by a group of people that didn't include Libby, but to whom he was more than willing to talk.

This was Phil's big moment, Charlotte thought, but he was in no way up to it. She was glad that Melanie was not there to bear witness. And she was not about to take responsibility for him herself.

Phil rambled on for several minutes in a disorganized way. All that his audience could hear clearly was, ". . . fifth claw . . . where's the ninth dragon?" and occasionally the word "fake."

At one point, he stumbled against the display form containing the white jade necklace, and the group around him let out a collective "Oh!" However, the well-anchored display form did not even sway.

Exhibit manager Barry Abrams pushed his way next to Phil. His fists were clenched at his sides, and for a moment Charlotte thought he was going to hit Phil. Instead he said, "Shut up, Stevenson!"

Phil sneered triumphantly. "I'm gonna tell Libby on you, Barry. I'm gonna tell 'em all." He waved his arm expansively toward the onlookers, and Barry grabbed it.

Libby finally joined them, just as the *Dispatch* photographer was snapping a picture of the group. The photographer took off as fast as he could through the crowd; Charlotte figured he wasn't supposed to take photographs in the art area at all, let alone photographs of any trouble.

Libby frowned and said something to Barry, who released Phil and followed the photographer. Then she smiled and spoke quietly to Phil. Linking her arm through his, she gently maneuvered him away from the group and out of the room. Uncharacteristically, it seemed to Charlotte, Phil accompanied her meekly.

The group that had watched Phil dispersed, and Charlotte went looking for Lou. She found her in the next exhibit room and excitedly recounted Phil's performance.

"What an obnoxious man," Lou said. "And your poor cousin Melanie. Is he always such a jerk?"

"As far as I've been able to tell, it's a constant condition," Charlotte said. "Melanie claims that Phil is simply too intense to have good social skills." Charlotte paused. "I've always thought it was because he was raised by wolves."

As they moved on to the next area in the show, Charlotte wished she had been able to understand more of what Phil had said.

"Especially the part about five claws and nine dragons," she told Lou. "Or was it nine claws and five dragons? Whatever it was, it had to do with his announcement that there's a fake here."

"I can't imagine that he's right—not with the credentials of this show."

"Still . . ."

"But even if he were, this was not the time to bring it

4

Philip Lyle Stevenson, Ph.D. in Oriental art history, was not just irritated. He was not just annoyed. He was not just angry. He was steamed. He was pissed. He was furious. And he was still a little bit drunk.

He jerked his car out of the Son of Heaven parking lot onto Broad Street going east, hit the horn at some hapless pedestrians, and screeched off down Broad. Ten minutes later he pulled into his suburban Bexley driveway and reached for the garage-door opener. Belatedly, he realized that the kids had been playing with it and had left it in the back seat. What the hell, he thought, and leaned on the horn.

Melanie came to the door with a dish towel in her hand. "Open the garage door," he roared. "Those kids of yours have lost the opener again."

Silently, Melanie turned, went back through the hall to the kitchen, opened the door to the attached garage, and pushed the button to start the automatic opener. Phil drove the car in, got out, slammed the door. "Go ahead," he gritted at Melanie. "Close the damned door."

Melanie pushed the button again and followed Phil into the kitchen. "What's wrong?" she asked. "I thought you were looking forward to your chat with the Chinese experts."

"Experts!" Phil snorted. "Some experts. When I pointed

out to them that there is something fishy about the jade necklace in Exhibit 138, they hustled me out of there. Wouldn't even listen to me."

"Oh, Phil," said Melanie. "I hope you didn't make a scene and embarrass Charlotte. She doesn't understand you anyway."

"Mel, I didn't intend to do anything. But when they wouldn't listen to me, I guess I got a little excited. Anyway, I need to look up some things in my study. Make me a pot of coffee, pronto. This may take a while."

Phil went upstairs, entered his study, and slumped into the desk chair. He got a pencil and a sheet of paper and started to list the books he would check for the information that would prove he was right about the jade necklace.

He yawned hugely, thought about getting one of the books down from the shelves, but didn't. He could find what he needed at Capital University's library or in the much more extensive Fine Arts Library at Ohio State. He was damned if he'd let those people get away with trying to put something over on *him* about his academic specialty.

The next morning the weather was dismal and Phil's spirits matched it. As he sat at the kitchen table drinking coffee, Melanie silently handed him the local section of the *Dispatch*. A picture of a radiant Libby Fox and the corporate sponsors of Son of Heaven was prominently featured with a lengthy article about the opening event. There was no mention of Phil's scene in the Outer Court. Shrugging, he drained his cup and left for the short, rainy drive to his office at Capital University.

He asked Mrs. Marchand, the department secretary, to take phone messages for him.

"I have some important research to complete right away, so I'm going to put the 'Do Not Disturb' sign on my door," he explained.

Mrs. Marchand smiled. She was used to Dr. Stevenson's getting carried away by what she called his "enthusiasms." She did hope, though, that not too many students would come by to complain when he wasn't available during his office hours.

Phil quickly went through the Chinese materials that were in his office. Not being completely satisfied with what he found, he decided to go on over to OSU to check some things in the Fine Arts Library.

When he stopped by Mrs. Marchand's desk to let her know he was leaving, she told him that he had had two phone calls, apparently from the same person, but that the caller had not left a message. She was about to mention the caller's unusual voice, a metallic sound that made it impossible to figure out gender, but he was half out the door. She quickly reminded him of his two o'clock Intro to Art History class and the departmental meeting that was scheduled for later.

Noting that it was ten o'clock, Phil decided he could find what he needed at OSU in plenty of time to make his class. As a former collegiate wrestler, he was used to skipping lunch in order to make the weight requirements. Besides, with this hangover, he didn't really feel like eating.

At that hour, Phil could be sure that the traffic would not be heavy on the freeways, even with the rain. So he headed his car west and then north to the OSU campus. He wove through the eastern edge of the campus along High Street and pulled into a parking garage, impatiently grabbing the ticket from the automatic machine.

He charged up High Street on foot to Sullivant Hall. Having visited the Fine Arts Library many times, he headed straight toward the stacks, then noted the special display for Son of Heaven at the front of the library. Squinting a bit, he quickly read all the titles and found that the particular book on Chinese art symbolism he wanted to see wasn't in the display. He turned and strode on to the stacks, where he located the item he wanted.

Seating himself at one of the long tables, he started to go through the book. Eventually, he sat back in his chair, smiling with smug satisfaction.

He copied the materials, then headed back to his car.

Following the class, Phil returned to his office. As he passed the open door of the department office, Mrs. Marchand waved to him and said, "There's a call on your line, Dr. Stevenson. Can you take it?" Phil nodded, walked quickly into his own office, closed the door, and picked up his phone.

His greeting was answered by a raspy, metallic genderless voice saying, "Stevenson?"

"Speaking. Who is this?"

The voice said, "I know you identified the fake in the Son of Heaven show last night. You have a good eye."

"Eyes had nothing to do with last night," Phil said. "This time it was brains, strictly brains."

"I just wanted you to know that you are absolutely right about the necklace being a fake."

"Of course I'm right." Phil could hear breathing on the line now. But the voice itself sounded computer-generated. Or perhaps the sound resulted from the kind of synthetic voice box used by people whose larynxes had been surgically removed.

Oblivious to what could be the feelings of such a person, he demanded, "What's the matter with your voice? Who are you? Why don't you identify yourself."

"That's simply not important."

When the caller did not continue, Phil said, "I know I'm right about the necklace. I've just spent several hours tracking down the information I need. All I have to do now is decide how I'm going to convince Libby and her flunky that they have a fake in their show."

"What would you say if I told you I could provide proof that the necklace is a fake?"

"What kind of proof?"

"Let's just call it 'incontrovertible' proof. I'll need to get some things together to show you. Why don't you meet me by the south door at Central around nine tonight. The show will be closed by that time and we can go in and look at the necklace while I show you my proof."

"I'd like an idea now of what you've got."

"Tonight. You'll see it tonight."

Phil agreed to the meeting.

"You said the south door?"

"That's right, the south door."

"How will I know you?" Phil asked.

"Just be there." And the caller hung up.

Phil pulled his calendar toward him, wrote "South Door" on the Monday-at-nine-o'clock line, and dropped it into his briefcase. With a sigh, he picked up the agenda for the department meeting and headed out the door.

Tuesday

When Lou and the rest of Columbus awoke the next morning, it was to sunlight sparkling off an ice-covered world. During the night, central Ohio had been hit by one of its almost yearly ice storms. Trees, bushes, parked cars, sidewalks, and pavement—everything that had been wet when the temperature abruptly dropped twenty degrees during the night—was now encased in an eighth-inch covering of ice.

Despite its beauty, it was a world that could be dangerous to navigate. Lou's drive to Central for her first day of once-a-week volunteer tour-guide duty was a frightening experience for her. Only the major streets had been salted, and she witnessed an unnerving batch of fender-benders before turning into Central's lot.

At the exhibit, Lou went to the old classroom that was serving as headquarters for volunteers and put on one of the black mandarin jackets with the gold imperial dragon printed on the back that had been designed for volunteers. After closing the jacket with the Velcro strip, she stuck her keys and wallet in the deep side pocket.

Lou then reported to her station at the turnstiles by the heavy red double doors. It looked as though all the Columbus groups scheduled for the day would be there, although the ice was causing some problems for the schools north of the city.

After seeing the 12-projector sound slide show that described the Chinese emperors' history and artifacts, twenty-five high school juniors came through the turnstiles. Lou led them through the red doors and brought them to a stop in front of the emperor's armor.

Conscientiously keeping the group moving through the Outer Court, the Inner Court, the Altar, the Temple, and the Tomb (deliberately kept ten degrees colder for effect), Lou, in just over an hour, led the group out the exit of the exhibit, down the stairs, and into the student coatroom.

She decided to step outside for a minute to see whether the ice was melting. Then she'd have to get back upstairs for her next group.

It hadn't melted at all. In fact, one of the sixth graders in an arriving group was taking advantage of the unsalted sidewalk east of the door to practice some fancy sliding maneuvers.

All of a sudden, he lost his balance and careened headfirst over a low privet hedge into ice-covered rhododendron bushes between the sidewalk and the south wall of the school. Wide-eyed, he teetered to his feet.

"Mrs. Burchfield, Mrs. Burchfield," he wailed. "There's a body in here!"

Looking startled, his teacher moved gingerly down the grass bordering the sidewalk. Lou couldn't help but follow the teacher toward the hedge.

The other sixth graders had been corralled by their chaperons and, over their protests, herded into the building. Their babble about a body had alerted the security guard, who immediately went outside. He joined the trio at the hedge and, with the others, looked down in disbelief.

The object of their gaze was the body of a man, probably in his late thirties, dressed in desert boots, jeans, and a navy-blue peacoat. A navy stocking cap had fallen off, exposing brown hair, cut short, and the cold pallor of his face.

"Oh, my God," Lou moaned. "That's Charlotte Sams's cousin's husband. That's Phil Stevenson."

The security guard took charge of the thoroughly frightened sixth grader, his teacher, and Lou, hustling them back into Central. Using the phone at the security desk, he quickly put through a call to the Columbus police and then placed the trio in the security headquarters room to await the arrival of the officers. A walkie-talkie call had brought four more security guards to block off the area where the body lay.

In the security office, sixth grader Danny O'Neill sat with the two women. None of them had had any experience with dead bodies before. Danny was making a determined effort to appear nonchalant, but his eyes were suspiciously shiny. Lou and Mrs. Burchfield were not in much better shape.

Pulling herself together, Lou said, "We all need some sugar in our systems. I'll go get us some hot chocolate, okay?" Doleful nods indicated that might be a good idea.

After telling the security guard she was going to the volunteers' lounge, Lou set off down the hall. The chocolate could wait. She found pay phones outside the gift shop.

"Hello?"

"Char," Lou said urgently, "I'm going to be late meeting you for lunch. Just wait for me and I'll be there as soon as I can. You won't believe what's happened."

"Lou, what—?"

"I can't talk now. I'll tell you everything later."

"But Lou—"

"Later, Char." And then she hung up.

Charlotte and Lou, each carrying a tray, dropped into seats under one of the ficus trees at the Lane Avenue Market. Since it was almost two o'clock, the Upper Arlington high school students who regularly came here for lunch had cleared out, so the usual lunchtime din had subsided.

"Oh, look," said Lou, "the Indian place on the far side of the market has finally opened."

"How can you talk about that right now?" Charlotte demanded. "Tell me more about Phil."

Lou obligingly continued to describe the events that had preceded her call to Charlotte's office, which she had begun while they were in line getting their lunches.

"When I got back to the security room with the hot chocolate about ten or fifteen minutes later, the police had arrived. There were two plainclothes detectives talking with Danny and Mrs. Burchfield. She pointed to me and said to one of the detectives, 'She's the one who knew the body.' The cops looked at me with funny expressions."

"I'll bet," said Charlotte.

"Actually, I think they were annoyed that I hadn't been in the room when they got there. Other officers were taking photographs and measurements, but they hadn't checked Phil's body for identification yet. It seems they had to get the pictures taken before they could move him. One of the detectives, Jefferson Barnes, asked me who I thought the body was."

"Jefferson Barnes? Isn't he one of the group that sued the city for race discrimination in promotions?"

"Oh, I didn't think of that, but you know, you may be right. He is black, and his name did sound familiar. Anyway, I told Barnes that I thought the dead man was Phil Stevenson and explained who he was and how I knew him. Actually, I don't think I made him sound as obnoxious as he is. I mean, was. But I did tell him about Phil's little scene at the gala."

"I wonder if Melanie knows yet," Charlotte said.

"Then one of the uniformed officers came in with a wallet that had been on the body and announced to the detectives that the deceased had been there at least overnight," Lou continued. "And of course the identification in the wallet indicated I was right. It was Philip Stevenson."

"If he still had his wallet, it couldn't have been a robbery," Charlotte pointed out. "Unless the thief was scared off for some reason. Maybe somebody deliberately murdered him."

"I didn't see any blood, Char. I think you're jumping to conclusions to assume that he was murdered. He might simply have fallen on the ice, bashed his head, and then froze to death."

"But why was he at Central anyway?" Charlotte wondered, looking doubtful. She answered herself. "Maybe he was there to check out the fake he announced at the gala. What did the detectives say about him having mentioned a fake?" she asked Lou.

"Well, you know how they are, Charlotte. They were very noncommittal about everything. Besides, they weren't at the event to actually hear Phil. Or to see his dreadful behavior. I suppose we'll just have to watch the news tonight to find out when and how he died."

"Poor Melanie. And then there are the kids to think about."

"How many did she and Phil have?"

"Three. There's Lionel and the two girls, Jade and Chrysanthemum."

"You're kidding."

"Nope."

"Phil Stevenson named his daughters Jade and Chrysanthemum?"

"Fits in nicely with his Oriental-art background, don't you think?" Charlotte said with elaborate innocence.

"I think it fits in with child abuse."

"I know what you mean. The kids aren't too bad, really, considering they've had Phil for a father. Tyler calls them dorky, though."

"That's better than using their given names."

"But who cares about names, anyway? There are probably lots of people who think Walt and I were crazy to name our kid Tyler."

"And I get lots of mail for 'Mr.' Lou Toreson. But I'd hate to be named Chrysanthemum."

"She seems to go by 'Chrys' now. Anyway, I'm sure Phil was responsible for those names and everything else about their marriage. Melanie won't know how to act, now that Phil's not around to tell her."

Lou wasn't overly sympathetic. "It was her own choice to live that way, Char. I suppose supporting three children after being intimidated out of any skills or talents that you might have had is a scary proposition. But now she won't have any choice."

Then Lou brightened. "On the other hand, maybe Phil had lots of insurance and Melanie did him in. Or maybe he didn't have any insurance and she still did him in."

"You're talking about my cousin here."

"But don't the police always look first at family members when a death seems suspicious?" Lou asked.

"I guess so. But you've met Melanie. Isn't it pretty hard to imagine that she could have anything to do with murder?"

"It's the meek ones you've got to watch."

"Well, she's meek, all right. But I really am curious about why Phil ended up dead."

"We all end up that way, Charlotte."

"I'm serious. I haven't known all that many people who have died. Especially so soon after they've made fools of themselves."

"Perhaps you don't know all that many foolish people. Or perhaps you're just not old enough yet," Lou laughed.

7

That evening Charlotte sat in Melanie Stevenson's spotless kitchen. Across the table sat a mourning Melanie who seemed somehow smaller than Charlotte remembered. The three Stevenson grade-schoolers were upstairs.

Absently, Melanie used a dishcloth to wipe that portion of the already clean table in front of her as she talked with Charlotte about her husband's death.

Given how dependent on Phil Melanie had seemed, Charlotte had expected to find her devastated. Prostrate with grief, as they say. But other than her reddened eyes and a certain absentmindedness, Melanie seemed pretty stable.

It was Charlotte who was uncomfortable. By this time she had said the usual consoling things one says to a bereaved spouse, sincerely feeling sorry for her cousin and her children. But try as she might, she couldn't work up any emotion for Phil himself. The conversation seemed to call for some expression of praise for him. But she found she couldn't do it. Hypocrisy was not her strong suit.

Luckily, a neighbor came to the back door to say she was sorry to hear on the radio about Phil's death and to ask whether there was anything she could do for Melanie. Upon learning that Charlotte was family, the neighbor said she figured Melanie was in good hands and quickly left. When Charlotte and Melanie resumed their conversation, the heat was off Charlotte to say anything pleasant about Phil. Instead, she asked about funeral plans.

"The police still have the body. They'll keep it until after the autopsy," Melanie answered. "They told me I don't have any choice about whether they do an autopsy since he had what they call an 'unattended' death and wasn't under a doctor's care."

"Don't you *want* to find out what Phil died from?"

"Well, the way the police have been treating me, you'd think I *murdered* Phil." At this point Melanie's eyes filled with tears and she dabbed at them with the cloth she had been using to clean the table.

"Did they tell you they thought he had been murdered?"

"They haven't told me anything. But I do."

"Do what?"

"Think Phil was murdered." Melanie looked totally miserable. "He was in good shape, Charlotte. He ran five miles a day, and sometimes he worked out in one of the gyms at Capital. He liked to show up the college kids."

Ah, there's the Phil I knew, thought Charlotte.

"And last week he had his yearly physical and the doctor told him he was in 'spectacular' shape. Phil was proud of that."

"I'm sure he was," Charlotte said. She had read that grief and feelings of helplessness often drove the loved ones of people who died suddenly to attribute the deaths to foul play. With some it became an obsession and interfered with working through the grief. So it seemed cruel to encourage Melanie to think along those lines. Better to let the autopsy settle the question.

Still, she couldn't resist asking why Phil had been at Central.

Melanie said she had no idea. "I didn't know *where* he was. I was worried when it got late and he still hadn't called. He's always very conscientious about calling when he has to work all night at the office."

Charlotte was startled. How many art historians have to

work around the clock? she wondered suspiciously. How big could the demand *be* for all-night identification of art work?

Melanie was explaining that she would have the funeral in Phil's Pennsylvania hometown. "But I'd like to have a memorial service here."

"That sounds nice."

Melanie looked sad. "I know you and Phil didn't get along, Charlotte, but he was wonderful at his job. He was important at Capital, and to local art organizations, too."

"I'm sure he was, Melanie."

"Those people will need some service to mark his passing and to mourn for him."

"Right." Charlotte wondered if they were talking about the same person.

"How are the kids taking this?"

"How do you *think* they're taking it?" Melanie said sharply. Both of them were surprised at her tone and Melanie quickly said, "Oh, I'm sorry, Charlotte. It's so hard for me to stay on an even keel right now." She wiped the clean table again with her tear-stained cloth. "The kids are doing okay. They'll be all right."

"Of course they will, Mel. And you don't have to apologize for being upset. Sometimes I ask dumb questions. It comes from my job—having to interview people all the time. I think you have amazing self-control for a situation like this."

They talked a short while longer, then Charlotte left. At home, she told Walt about Melanie's theory that Phil was murdered. Walt didn't buy it.

"Exercise and a good physical aren't any guarantees," he said. "You hear all the time about people dropping dead the day after they passed a physical."

"You're just looking for something to reinforce your re-fusal to exercise," she said, reviving an old argument.

"Maybe. You know I've always agreed with that comedian who said he never exercised because he was afraid he would drop his cigarette and spill his drink."

Charlotte chuckled with him, despite the fact that she was

convinced she would die if she stopped exercising and was afraid Walt could go at any moment because he had never *started.*

"Well, no matter what he died of, Phil was in rare form when he announced a fake at the gala."

"Just sounds like the same old loudmouthed Stevenson to me."

"Right, but there's no denying that the dragons on the jade necklace were different from those on the other pieces."

"So?"

"So I'm wondering whether Phil was right about there being a fake and whether I can write an article on all this."

"Maybe so, but can we talk about this tomorrow? If lack of exercise won't kill me, lack of sleep definitely will."

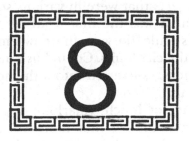

C harlotte was still wondering how to find out whether the necklace was authentic when she took her walk early the next morning. By the time she drove to her office, she had decided to start her investigation by learning about jade and the significance of dragons on Chinese jewelry.

The lights were on in the two-room office, but no one was there. On the desk in the outer room, Claudia had left a note that she was off doing errands that Charlotte had assigned and that Conor Ennis had called to cancel his interview that afternoon.

Damn. Ennis was the saxophone player Charlotte was writing about, and this was the third interview he had canceled in as many days. Why would a musician be so reluctant to talk with her? she wondered. Maybe it was no more complicated than that he was busy. But Charlotte had yet to meet a performer who was not anxious to get the free publicity an article in *Ohio Blue Note* could generate. It seemed odd that he should be so uncooperative.

Maybe, Charlotte thought, she should just drop in at his studio, catch Ennis unaware, and hope he'd not be able to turn her down for the interview once she was in front of him.

The rest of the morning was filled with phone calls to get information for several articles she was contemplating, and working on projects that were in various stages of completion. Among them was the first draft of an article about what the state should do with the now empty Ohio Penitentiary within the city limits. Columbus's mayor, she wrote, had suggested it be converted into a theme park. She had not made that up.

Before leaving for lunch, Charlotte dug out the Son of Heaven exhibition catalog that Lou had insisted she buy weeks ago and took it with her to a nearby fast-food place. Over a baked potato, she examined the lavishly illustrated, 200-page volume that contained color photographs of many of the items exhibited.

Unfortunately, the necklace in question was not among the pieces pictured, and there was only a brief mention of it in the text:

> Exhibit 138. Imperial jade necklace, consisting of nine plaques, carved with dragons, clouds, and mountains.
> Ming (before 1371), First Emperor Chu' Yüanchang, Chengjuo City Museum (Gift of the Empress Dowager Tzu Hsi)

She couldn't find any reference in the catalog to the desirability of having nine five-clawed dragons either.

Back at the office, Charlotte paced excitedly around the perimeter of the inner room, glad that Claudia Pepperdine was not there to witness her typical behavior at this stage of an article. She loved this phase, when the emphasis was on discovery. Later would come the more tedious writing phase, after her curiosity had been satisfied and she had to struggle to say everything just right.

Over the years, she had decided that there really was very little new under the sun and that whatever she needed to know was already known by somebody or was in some reference book somewhere. The trick was to locate that person or reference in time for the information to still be valuable to her.

Lou, Charlotte remembered, had not believed there could be a fake in the Son of Heaven show because of all the scholars involved in putting on the show. One scholar she had mentioned was an art history professor from Ohio State, Joy Montgomery, who had lectured to the volunteers but was not really part of the Son of Heaven show.

What was remarkable about Montgomery, Lou had told Charlotte, was that she had seemed not only knowledgeable but also anxious that her audience actually learn from her presentation. A veteran of hundreds of lectures in which the speaker did not seem to realize the audience was even present, Lou had found Montgomery's attitude refreshing.

It took two tries, but Charlotte was able to reach Montgomery by phone in her OSU office that afternoon. She introduced herself as a local writer trying to learn about Chinese symbolism in art, but carefully avoided mentioning a potential article, the Son of Heaven show, or the necklace. Still, she managed to ask whether nine dragons with five claws on each foot had any special significance in Chinese art.

To her happy surprise, Montgomery explained right off that imperial items decorated with dragons typically had nine of them, all five-clawed.

The five-clawed dragon, she said, had been the emblem of imperial power since the reign of Emperor Kao Tsu of the Han dynasty in about 206 B.C. The scaly monster had been considered a divine animal, a symbol of vigilance and safeguard. And nine was the number most associated with the emperor.

Charlotte was furiously taking notes as fast as Montgomery spoke. "What about items that had fewer dragons or fewer than five claws on each foot?" she managed to ask.

Typically, they were not imperial, Montgomery said. Charlotte wanted to know exactly what that meant.

"It means that they would not have been used by the emperor."

"You said 'typically'," Charlotte pressed. "Does that mean that you know of exceptions?"

"Well, actually, I've never looked into the question of exceptions. You have to remember that only about one percent of Chinese antiquities have been excavated. So we're all just learning about them, no matter how well-versed any of us seems to be in Chinese art," Montgomery explained.

She then agreed to investigate whether there were known exceptions to what Charlotte had decided to call the nine five-claw dragon rule, and to let Charlotte know.

Charlotte spent an hour or so clipping articles from several publications—articles that contained ideas or information that she might need in future stories. About two hours past the time she would have met with Ennis, she dropped in at his studio, only to be told by his manager that he wasn't there.

"I thought he had canceled his meeting with you," the manager said.

Right. So much for the impromptu approach. Impulsively Charlotte drove back up High Street, past her office building to Whetstone Park, which contained a branch of the Columbus Metropolitan Library.

She was a library junkie. (Walt had long maintained that when she died, the library would build the Charlotte M. Sams Memorial Wing—financed entirely with her overdue-book fines.) The Whetstone branch was her favorite. It was not a particularly large library—although through it one had easy access to materials at all twenty-one branches of the Columbus system—but its staff was especially helpful.

A large metal sculpture set against the building depicted the outlines of a giant book lying open on its back, with three metal pages appearing to flap open in the air. The title of the work was "Reason Made Solid," and Charlotte had very strong feelings about that sculpture. It was so blasted *literal*. She considered it to be about as artful as the international symbols for men and women that labeled the doors of public rest rooms.

Nonetheless, she had to admit that books were reason made solid to her. Books had long had a physical effect on her. If she felt good, the books were almost physically exciting because they made all things seem possible. If she was upset, they had a calming effect. Charlotte invariably went to the library after she had a fight with Walt.

Today, jade was the order of business. She went directly to the library's periodical room to use the CD-ROM database system called InfoTrak II/Magazine Index Plus. The database indexed business materials, four hundred popular magazines and journals, and *The New York Times.*

She sat at an InfoTrak station, typed in her subject, j-a-d-e, and pressed the "search" key. A message that said "searching" appeared briefly, lest she think that her request was being ignored. Then the word JADE appeared with thirteen alphabetized subheadings below it.

Charlotte selected the "analysis" subheading and a single citation, for a five-year-old article in *Lapidary Journal,* appeared on screen. She pushed the "print" key and a small printer next to the computer printed out the citation.

After printing several more citations, but none that seemed exactly what she wanted, she switched subjects, looking this time for "jade art objects." Under that heading, the subheading "appreciation" yielded a citation for an article by Fred Ward called "Jade: Stone of Heaven" in a two-year-old *National Geographic.* Delighted at the similarity between the article's name and the art show's, she printed.

About ten minutes later, a smiling Charlotte drove home, the magazine article on the seat beside her.

C harlotte was so enthusiastic about her research on jade
that she skipped her walk the next morning in order to
organize her notes on the *National Geographic* article over
breakfast. She had to explain her presence at the breakfast
table to Walt, of course, who was relieved that she would
be writing and that he would still have the morning news-
papers to himself.

A phone call interrupted their conversation. Walt
groaned, assuming it was from an habitually late employee
who regularly called him at home to announce why he could
not make it to work before nine-thirty. But the call was from
Joy Montgomery.

Returning to the table after the call, Charlotte told Walt
she'd asked Montgomery to verify the nine five-claw dragon
rule.

"And she did, Walt," Charlotte crowed triumphantly.
"She said that she could find no exceptions among her
sources. The Chinese always used nine dragons, all of them
five-clawed, on items that were used by their emperors."

"How consistent of them," he said, reluctantly putting
down the paper. "So the necklace wasn't really used by an
emperor?"

"Nope. And I'm betting that's why Phil called it a fake."

"*Does* that make it a fake?"

"Well, maybe 'fake' is too strong a word. But at least it's not what the Son of Heaven show says it is. It's not imperial." She paused, considering. "Maybe it's not even jade."

"Why would you think that?"

"Because it's easy to fool people with jade. I know that in the last day or so I've learned enough about jade to decide I'll never buy any again for fear of being cheated."

"Funny, but I seem to think of myself as the major jade purchaser here."

Charlotte smiled. "And a wonderful job you've done of it, too," she said. Then she told him what she had learned from the *National Geographic* article.

"A Chinese myth says jade was given to the world by the storm god. He saved all humanity by forging a rainbow into jade axes and giving them to the humans just in the nick of time during some catastrophe."

"Anthropologists must have a whole category of 'just in the nick of time' myths," Walt interjected.

"Right. But the article said that no other culture has ever treated a substance with more esteem and devotion than the Chinese once reserved for nephrite."

"I thought we were talking about jade," Walt said.

"Nephrite is one of two kinds of 'real' jade, meaning what can legally be called jade."

"Trust the lawyers to get involved."

"There are lots of different jade look-alike stones called jade simulants. But real jade is either *nephrite* or *jadeite*," Charlotte explained. "Jadeite and nephrite are chemically different, having been formed by different combinations of chemicals, heat, and pressure. Both kinds occur in a variety of colors—green, red, lavender, and white, like the necklace."

She paused while Walt got up to get them more coffee.

"Okay, next question," he said, returning with the pot. "How do you tell real jade from the simulants? And nephrite from jadeite?"

"Apparently it's almost impossible—even for experts—

to tell real jade from a jade simulant just by looking. The same is true for distinguishing between nephrite and jadeite. But in that case, it helps to know where the piece came from. All old jade carvings from China are of nephrite because that's the only kind of jade China has, and jadeite wasn't even discovered until after 1850. Most jadeite comes from Burma, Guatemala, and Siberia. Nearly all of it becomes jewelry.

"The article says that in today's market, it's the bright-green jadeite that is highly prized, rather than the other, more delicate colors that nephrite comes in. Most of that bright-green jadeite comes from Burma. And, to complicate matters, that bright-green jadeite is called 'imperial' jade."

"Which is obviously a misnomer, right?" Walt said, surprising Charlotte with the closeness with which he had been following the story. "Since you just said that Chinese jade items used by any but the most recent emperors are of nephrite."

"That's right. Don't ask me to defend the labels relating to jade."

"Just tell me how you could find out whether the necklace is jade, Charlotte."

"Well, you'd have to do physical tests." She went on to explain what she'd learned about the tests.

When she had finished, Walt said, "That's more than I've ever wanted to know about jade in my life. You've outdone yourself this time, Charlotte."

Tyler slid into his seat at the table and reached for the cereal. His short blond hair looked dark and spiky from the shower.

"Who are you?" he said to Charlotte. "I don't usually have a mother until seven-thirty."

"That other woman was an imposter," she answered.

10

B y the time Charlotte reached Columbus Central early that afternoon, she had spent considerable time congratulating herself on having verified that a fake was part of a prestigious art show. She would have preferred to have been the one who had actually detected the fake in the first place, but those honors went to the dead Phil Stevenson.

Even so, she was going to make sure that it was she who broke the story in the local press. She envisioned selling an exclusive to the *Dispatch*, a longer piece to *Columbus Monthly*, and, possibly, some shorter pieces to several national art monthlies.

She had even convinced herself that exhibit manager Barry Abrams would welcome her inquiry into the necklace's authenticity. Things did not work out quite that way.

Charlotte was directed to Abrams's first-floor office by a volunteer wearing a mandarin jacket; Barry himself ushered her to a folding chair set up opposite his metal desk. The room's high ceiling and bank of windows across one wall were reminders that the office had previously been a classroom.

Barry assured her that he remembered her from the Son of Heaven dinner. Then he leaned back in his chair and asked, "Now what can I do for you? You sounded quite mysterious on the phone this morning, Ms. Sams."

"I just thought I should speak with you face-to-face about this matter, Mr. Abrams," Charlotte said.

"Call me Barry, please," he said, smiling.

"All right, Barry," said Charlotte. "You see, I have reason to believe that the Ming white jade necklace you are displaying in the Son of Heaven exhibit, number 138, is not authentic."

Barry stopped smiling and sat up abruptly in his chair. He looked stunned.

Finally, he laughed incredulously. "You can't be serious. What possible reason could you have for believing that?"

Patiently, Charlotte explained her case. Barry, of course, asked her what her interest was in all this and was not pleased to find out that she was a writer. He interrupted frequently to counter what she was saying about the necklace.

He told her that he had never heard of any nine five-claw dragon rule, but did allow that perhaps that didn't mean much, since his area of expertise was not in art history but in displaying and promoting art. But he pointed out that his expertise gave him a closer relationship to art history than hers did.

"You are," he stated ungraciously, "an art amateur."

The professional credentials of everyone connected with the show were impeccable, according to Abrams. It was preposterous to think that any one of them had misrepresented an item in the show, purposefully or mistakenly.

"I'm just saying that the authenticity of the necklace bears investigating," Charlotte said. "I'm not saying I know who is responsible for any problem. If your professionals are so far above reproach, perhaps a worker who packed the items for shipment simply packed the wrong thing."

"Impossible!" Abrams sprang out of his chair and stood right in front of Charlotte. She was reminded of how furious he had been at Phil at the gala.

"The art works were crated under curatorial supervision in both China and Seattle. And security has been very tight ever since they have been in this country." Barry's voice rose as he spoke. "I am not at liberty to describe our security arrangements here at Central to you. But, believe me, they are quite effective."

Charlotte considered this last part to be a bit patronizing and bristled. "The tightness of security is logically irrelevant to the issue of the necklace's authenticity," she retorted. "The necklace either is or is not what it is represented to be. Its violation of the nine five-claw dragon rule is evidence enough that it may be a fraud."

She paused to gauge Barry's reaction. He remained silent, looking at her warily.

"I know of some safe ways to test the necklace," she went on. "And frankly, Mr. Abrams, I'd think you'd be quite anxious to confirm the authenticity of any item about which there is the slightest question."

"But you are the only one who has raised 'the slightest question.'"

"You're forgetting Phil Stevenson," she couldn't resist saying.

Barry stiffened. "Look, lady. Let me tell you this: There are few in Columbus's art community who are mourning Stevenson's death. He was one obnoxious SOB."

"That may be, but Oriental art was his specialty," Charlotte reminded him. "I can't understand why you are so reluctant to act on Phil's and my information."

"Because I think it is utterly without merit," Barry said sharply. "You'll have to forgive me if I don't jump at the chance to embarrass the entire Son of Heaven staff, the show's sponsors, and our Chinese colleagues on the strength of the opinions of a non-expert. And, frankly, I'm beginning to wonder about *your* motives."

Barry stayed on the offensive and proceeded to accuse Charlotte of everything from being in cahoots with the political enemies of the politicians who supported the show (she could have had her pick: Mayor Rinehart was a Republican; Governor Celeste was a Democrat) to trying to create an international incident between China and the United States.

Finally she had had enough. She abruptly thanked Abrams for his time and left his office. As she walked down the hall, she could hear him behind her, shouting that he'd sue if he saw any of this in print.

Once in her car, she took a few moments to make notes on her meeting in a notebook she always kept handy. Then she decided to call on Libby Fox at the art museum. What did she have to lose?

Unfortunately, Libby was not in. The best Charlotte could do was make an appointment for the next morning.

Back in her office, she got out her university phone directory, and before the afternoon was over, she knew quite a bit about what resources were available at Ohio State to help determine whether the necklace was jade—all without revealing the exact object whose composition she was investigating. It had taken some tricky talking, but she didn't want anyone else questioning the authenticity of the necklace until they read *her* story in the *Dispatch*.

Both the chemistry and geology departments would be able to help, but all of the tests they routinely used were destructive tests. Those, of course, were out of the question because they would have damaged the necklace.

So who ran tests on beautiful objects that would not damage the objects themselves? she wondered. Finally, she called a jewelry store that made custom items. She talked with an Angela Fitzpatrick, who said she was a gemologist and who sounded knowledgeable.

Angela offered some interesting insights on jade. For instance, she said that it is the color and any carving on jade that account for its value, not merely the fact that it is jade. She told Charlotte that she owned a piece of jade that was about the size of a brick. A jade "brick" sounded wondrous, but Angela pointed out that since there was no carving on her "brick" and that it was a dull rather than lustrous green, it really wasn't worth very much. The color of jade is crucial to its value, Angela said, mentioning a sale in Burma a couple of years ago at which a piece of green jadeite the size of a man's fist had sold for over a million dollars.

When they discussed tests, Angela referred Charlotte back to OSU—this time to the physics department, which used spectrometry. Charlotte wondered why the chemistry and geology departments had not referred her to the physics department in the first place, and finally chalked it up to academic independence, or competition, or carelessness. She really didn't mind having had to go through Angela to get to the correct department, since she had found out such interesting information on jade in the process.

The head of the physics department verified that spectrometry could help to safely identify what the necklace was made of and recommended a physicist on the faculty who might be willing to run the test. He told Charlotte the department owned a Portable Instantaneous Display and Analysis Spectrometer (PIDAS), so the machine could be brought to the necklace rather than the necklace having to be brought to the machine. Perfect.

As she hung up, the phone rang. "So how did it go with Abrams?" Walt asked innocently.

"Miserably," Charlotte answered and then described her meeting.

"Maybe it was a little optimistic to expect him to immediately take action about the necklace," Walt suggested.

"Or maybe he's just protecting the show."

"Why don't you give the guy some time, Charlotte? Once he gets over his surprise, he might become less defensive and actually have the necklace tested."

"You didn't hear how angry he was, Walt."

"No, but I know that you've had several days to get used to this idea that the necklace could be a fake."

"It was easy."

"Because you don't have anything to lose if it is. Abrams does, so you can't very well blame him for being surprised and upset."

"Whose side are you on, Walt?"

"Yours, of course. But you always get so obsessive about your projects when they're new. Give him a chance to catch up with your thinking."

"He's probably plotting right now how to stop my story," Charlotte said ruefully.

"Did you see the article in this morning's paper about Phil? It talks a lot about his college wrestling career. I had forgotten that he was so illustrious."

"Some other wrestler probably dropped him on his head," Charlotte snorted.

The next morning, she met with Libby to explain her concerns about the necklace. After her experience with Barry, she found Libby to be curiously receptive. The curator stressed that she was interested in maintaining the integrity of the show and agreed to try to talk Barry into having the test run. If she was successful, she'd ask Charlotte to make the necessary arrangements with the physicist at Ohio State. She did not have to caution Charlotte to keep the story to herself in the meantime.

C harlotte had spent most of the weekend cooking in order to take her mind off her impatience for Monday and the necklace test. Tyler, who had never seen his mother spend so much time in the kitchen, asked her if she was writing a cookbook.

Monday evening was clear. There were no reminders of the ice storm that had bejeweled the city exactly a week before. Arriving at Central for the after-hours test of the necklace that Libby Fox had talked Barry Abrams into, Charlotte couldn't resist approaching the building from the south—the side of the building on which Phil Stevenson's body had been discovered.

The south door was locked, so she went around to the front entrance and went in as the last visitors to the show were being ushered out. After she had explained to one of the omnipresent volunteers in a mandarin jacket why she was there, the volunteer said, "Oh, yes. Dr. Fox told us not to lock up until you were inside. But I thought there was to be a gentleman with you."

Charlotte explained that Dr. Clayton Armstrong and his graduate student would be along soon. "You'll know it's them because they'll be carrying some heavy equipment."

The volunteer told them that Libby expected them to meet her in Barry's office.

On the way, Charlotte abruptly ducked into the darkened room where the dinner had been held. She inched her way down the slope toward the display cases. Ahead lay the art works in cases whose lights were still on, making eerie pools of illumination in the otherwise dark and silent hall.

"Perhaps I can help you," came a voice behind her. Charlotte gasped and turned with a jerk.

Barry stood there, smiling sourly at her.

"I just wanted to see how easy it would be for someone to have gotten close to the necklace after the show was closed for the night," Charlotte explained lamely.

"Please stand still," Barry said. "Don't move."

She watched as he walked back up the slope, opened the door, and spoke briefly to someone outside. Then he returned to Charlotte.

"The necklace is this way," he told her, unnecessarily, since she knew as well as he where the necklace was displayed.

This man thinks I'm an idiot, Charlotte thought crossly as she followed him.

On the way, Barry explained that she had set off security alarms from the moment she had entered the room.

"But I didn't touch anything, and I didn't hear any alarms," Charlotte said.

"You didn't have to. There are movement sensors throughout this room that detect when someone is here, regardless of whether they touch any of the cases. You didn't hear the alarms because they don't ring in here. We wouldn't want to alert a thief that we knew he was here. The alarms ring in the security office down the hall and in the offices of Acme Security up on High Street. I've just told my assistant to turn off the alarms and to tell Acme that everything is under control.

"It is, isn't it?" he asked, pausing to look at her. "You're not going to slug me and grab the necklace, are you?"

"Not likely," Charlotte said, fervently hoping that Barry would trip in the dark.

The necklace lay shimmering in the light of its display case, resting on a black velvet stand that made the white necklace look even whiter.

It seems so innocent, she thought. She peered closer, counting, to make certain that she hadn't made some dreadful mistake.

There were still only eight dragons and only four claws on each white dragon foot.

She and Abrams moved to the back of the case, and Barry used the fingertips of both hands to trace the edges of a panel fitted flush with the case's back. Then he put his right hand into his jacket pocket and drew out a very thin metal rod about five inches long.

Charlotte expected him to use the tool as a mini-crowbar to pry off the back panel. Instead he worked it as a screwdriver to remove several tiny screws that held the panel in place. She could see that one end of the rod had been flattened to a very fine, knifelike edge.

"I've never seen a tool like that," said Charlotte, thinking that her son would love such an exotic item.

"It was designed and made specially for this exhibit. Part of the security. There are not supposed to be many items that could accomplish this task with the panel screws—certainly no conventional screwdriver could," Barry explained.

When he had removed six screws, he held the panel in place with his left hand while he slipped the tool back into his pocket with his right. Then he let the panel fall into his hands, lifted it completely out, and set it on the floor against the bottom of the stand.

Charlotte peered into the lighted case and Barry said sharply, "Don't touch anything."

Then he carefully reached inside the case and brought out the necklace still on its stand. Charlotte could see that it was the stand that he was actually holding, with the necklace carefully balanced on top.

"I'm leaving it on the stand because we mustn't put any stress on the necklace itself. If we held it instead of the stand, or held the necklace by its clasp, for instance, its own weight might break it," Barry explained.

They walked to his office, with Charlotte carefully holding the doors open for the man with the necklace.

Libby was seated behind Barry's desk, chatting with a tall bespectacled man in his late fifties. If Barry minded that she seemed to have taken over his office, he didn't show it. Charlotte assumed the older man must be the physicist Clayton Armstrong and that the deferential, much younger man sitting next to him was his graduate assistant.

Barry put the stand on the desk, and Libby made introductions all around. The graduate student's name was Ted Zyzanski.

"Clayton has been telling me about the test he's going to run on our necklace, Barry," Libby said. "If you don't mind, Clayton, would you please tell Barry and Charlotte about it?"

The physicist told the group that he and Ted would use spectrometry to analyze the necklace. They had brought with them a PIDAS, which measured light reflected from the surface of a mineral to create a wavelength "signature" that is unique to that particular mineral. If the signature of the necklace matched the established signature for nephrite or jadeite, they would pronounce the necklace jade. If it didn't match, then they would try to match it with the signature of another material.

Before long, Ted had set up the PIDAS on the desk, explaining that what was new about this spectrometer was its portability. Before the Jet Propulsion Laboratory in California invented this contraption, which weighed only about seventy pounds, anything to be analyzed by spectrometry had to be brought to a large laboratory spectrometer—which was, of course, too risky to do with some items, such as art works, because they could be damaged in transit. Now the PIDAS could be brought to the material being analyzed.

Armstrong positioned the necklace on its stand under the light source supplied by the PIDAS and then turned out the overhead lights in the office. He turned on the PIDAS and looked in the eyepiece for the telltale band of colored light that showed the range of light reflected and absorbed by the surface of the necklace. In a few moments, the PIDAS had converted the colored band to electronic impulses that were printed as a line graph on a computer tape that came out the rear of the PIDAS.

Armstrong tore off the printout and studied it intently. This was the signature of the material that composed the necklace. He held it next to the signatures of jadeite and nephrite in the reference book Zyzanski had laid open on the desk.

Finally he looked up. "Well, whatever else it is," he said, "this necklace isn't jade."

"Of course I'm going to write about this," Charlotte stated flatly.

"But that will only embarrass the Son of Heaven show and the whole city," Libby said, distressed. "Why would you want to do that?"

"I don't want to embarrass anybody. But this is an interesting story, and the public has a right to know about the art shows they pay to see. Especially the art shows that are put on with public money."

Barry Abrams held the computer tape on which the necklace's signature was printed, staring at it as though he could will it to divulge its secrets. Armstrong and Zyzanski were packing up the PIDAS.

Libby tried again to talk Charlotte out of writing about the necklace, but was making no headway.

To Libby, Armstrong said, "Since you don't want this made public, why did you agree to have the test run on the necklace?"

"Yes, Libby," Barry said bitterly. "I'd really like to know why you agreed to let this meddler set up a test."

"Barry," Libby said sharply, "it's true that Charlotte came to me with intriguing evidence. But I already knew something was strange about that necklace. After Phil Stevenson made his accusations, I went back to the museum to look at the Alliance Insurance documents on the necklace. The insurance pictures showed that when the exhibit was assembled in China, the dragons were five-clawed and the ninth dragon was on the reverse of one of the small pieces."

Charlotte asked Barry to turn over the necklace.

Libby said, "Don't bother. I've already checked, and it's not there. That's why I've been anxious myself to find out about this necklace."

Nonetheless, Barry turned over the necklace, which revealed the smooth backsides of the pieces, which everyone in the room now knew were something other than jade. No dragon showed its claws of any number.

"How could this have happened?" Barry asked.

"I don't know," Libby said. "You were in charge of setting up the show, Barry. I could ask you the same question."

Barry, looking ill, sat down on one of the folding chairs facing his desk. Libby turned back toward Charlotte.

"Maybe there's some arrangement we can make that will protect the show *and* your right to write about the necklace," she said. "How about if we promise you exclusive rights to the story and our complete cooperation in writing it? In return, you would not write and sell the story until after the show closes in September."

"But the public has a right to know when an art object is not authentic," Charlotte insisted.

"Well, we'll take the necklace out of the show. Then no one will be deceived, and your journalistic conscience will be clear. The show won't be damaged and you'll still get your story—once the show can't be hurt. And the story will be better because we'll be sharing whatever information we have about the necklace with you."

Libby spoke softly and persuasively, but the civilized effect was broken by Barry. "We're not likely to be very helpful if you write the story now, you know," he threatened.

"I don't like the idea of sitting on the news . . ."

"It's not exactly the Pentagon Papers story," said Barry. "And you're not exactly Woodward and Bernstein."

He was right about that, Charlotte knew. The story was interesting but until she could uncover how the authentic necklace was taken out of the show and the fake put in, it wasn't a real blockbuster. To learn all that, she'd need Libby's cooperation and maybe Barry's, too.

Charlotte finally agreed not to write about the necklace until after the show closed. In exchange, Barry and Libby agreed not to discuss the necklace with any other writers or reporters and promised their total cooperation when she did get to write the story.

Charlotte had almost forgotten that Armstrong and Zyzanski were still in the room, but the two academics had been listening intently to the negotiations. They, too, had to be sworn to secrecy.

As they were getting ready to leave, Charlotte mentioned casually that she was pretty impressed that Phil had been able to detect the fake necklace the first time he had seen it, still displayed in its case.

"Especially since he was half-drunk at the time," Barry said. "Maybe it was easy for him to pick out the necklace because he put it there."

The allegation caught Charlotte off-guard. More for Melanie's sake than Phil's, she managed to say, "Well, it's always easy to blame somebody who can't defend himself."

In her usual role as peacemaker, Libby said something about "Phil's tragic death." Charlotte took that opportunity to ask whether either she or Barry knew why Phil had been at Central the night before his body was discovered.

Both said they had no idea. Libby explained that she had been making fund-raising telephone calls from her museum office. Charlotte turned to Barry, expectantly.

"I was tied up all evening in my office doing Son of Heaven paperwork last Monday," he said. "I certainly hadn't made an appointment to see Philip bloody Stevenson. After the scene he made, I thought we would be lucky if we never saw him again."

At home later, Charlotte began telling Walt and Tyler about the necklace being made of something other than jade. She did not get far before being interrupted by Melanie Stevenson, telephoning with the results of another test: the autopsy on Phil's body. Charlotte took the call in the kitchen, pulling a chair toward the wall phone and settling in for what she imagined would be a long conversation. She was right.

"They say it was a heart attack, Charlotte, but you know what I think of that," Melanie said.

"Who, exactly, said it was a heart attack?"

Melanie explained that Detective Barnes had arrived at the Stevenson house late that afternoon, bringing the report's confirmation that Phil had died of a heart attack. He told her the time of death had been placed between eight and ten the night before his body had been discovered at Columbus Central.

"Well, at least now you know the truth, Mel," Charlotte said.

"The truth? I'll *never* believe Phil had a heart attack," Melanie insisted.

"But I haven't heard of many autopsy reports being wrong. After you give yourself more time, I bet things make a lot more sense to you."

"Never. Somebody killed him and just made it look like a heart attack. Probably because he was right about there being a fake in that Chinese art show," she stated positively.

Resisting the temptation to tell Melanie about the test run on the necklace, Charlotte asked, "Exactly *who* killed him, Mel? And how?"

"How would I know? Maybe they gave him something that just made it look like he died of a heart attack. But I'm right about him being murdered. I'm sure of it, and I want you to find out who killed him."

"You're kidding!"

"Come on, Charlotte. You do research for your articles. You're good at figuring things out. You'll be able to find out who killed Phil and how it looked like a heart attack."

"Do you know what kind of research I do? The article I'm working on now is about a saxophone player. That's a long way from investigating a murder."

"See! Even you think Phil was murdered."

"I do not, and you know it!" Who was this person? Charlotte wondered. Phil had been dead only a week and already Melanie seemed like a different person. Charlotte was beginning to think she liked her better as a mouse. "Besides," she added, "even if I did think he was murdered, I wouldn't know how to prove it."

"But you're smart, Charlotte. You know how to find out all kinds of things. And the plain truth is, I don't know who else to turn to."

And so it went, until Melanie wore Charlotte down and she agreed to ask some questions. She didn't for a minute think Phil had been murdered, but she knew she'd need more information about his accusations for her articles. Asking some questions at Melanie's request would help her get it.

Before hanging up, Melanie said she had scheduled Phil's funeral for Thursday in Pennsylvania and the memorial service for the following Sunday afternoon in Columbus.

Charlotte casually told Walt and Ty that she was humoring Melanie by agreeing to ask some questions about Phil's death. She was determined not to play private investigator. In fact, the more she thought about it, the sillier the whole idea seemed. The only mitigating fact was that she actually had been successful in tracking down a fake in an art show. Was that enough to make her a sleuth? Probably not.

It was almost two in the morning when the phone rang, jarring Charlotte out of a sound sleep. She grabbed the phone off the small table next to her side of the bed. Her "hello" was not cordial.

Neither was the sound emanating from the receiver in her hand. "Are you listening?"

She nearly dropped the phone. It was a deep-pitched, hoarse, metallic voice that she would have assumed was machine-generated had she not been able to hear breathing.

"I just want to make sure you understand that people who stick their noses in where they don't belong sometimes get them cut off," it wheezed.

"What?"

"That's all. Just lay off, or you may lose your own nose."

The line went dead, and Charlotte put the receiver back in its cradle, her heart pounding. Then, almost without thinking, she ran downstairs and checked to see that all the doors and windows were locked.

Back upstairs, she sat on the bed in the dark bedroom and stared at the telephone. Because of the metallic voice, she felt as if she'd been threatened by Darth Vader. She considered waking Walt but couldn't think of anything he could do.

Lose her nose? The call had succeeded in frightening her, even though she couldn't make much sense of it. Who would want to hurt her? And just where was she poking her nose in that it didn't belong? On occasion, people were upset at an article she wrote, but she hadn't written about anything very controversial for some time. Conor Ennis might be avoiding her, but she had trouble imagining the musician making phone threats in the middle of the night.

That left the fake necklace business. If the caller had threatened her to keep her from investigating the necklace, he—or she—was too late. After the test in Barry Abrams's office, she wasn't the only one who knew the necklace was not authentic. And Clayton Armstrong could call the Son of Heaven staff as well as Charlotte, once he figured out what the necklace was really made of.

Maybe the fact that she was threatened after the test had been run meant that the caller did not know about the test. So he thought she was the only one who knew about the fake. Or perhaps he knew about the test but also knew she had just agreed to help Melanie look for a killer. Maybe he *was* the killer.

Charlotte would have preferred he had called Melanie.

14

Tuesday

Charlotte was pacing around her office again, wondering how to get started asking questions regarding the fake necklace and Phil Stevenson's accusations. Far from deterring her, the previous night's threatening phone call had only increased her determination to find out what she needed for her articles and, incidentally, to find out what she could about Phil's death—assuming there was anything to find out. She'd just have to be careful.

She didn't exactly know what to do next. Melanie had claimed Phil was killed to shut him up about the fake necklace. Charlotte didn't know who else knew what Phil had known. Who had heard Phil make his allegations at the gala? she wondered.

She dug the *Dispatch* story out of a stack of articles waiting to be filed by Claudia. Perhaps, Charlotte thought, looking at the height of the stack, I should stop giving Claudia so many assignments outside the office.

The article included a photograph of a smiling Libby Fox surrounded by the Son of Heaven show's corporate sponsors. Charlotte remembered another photograph being taken while Phil was acting up. The credit line under the story's photograph read, "*Dispatch* photo by Todd McClanahan."

She called the *Dispatch*, was put through to McClanahan,

and got him to agree to let her stop by on her lunch hour to take a look at his unpublished prints of that night. When she got there, he even let her keep one in which she appeared—the one he had snapped when Phil was talking about the fake.

That afternoon she phoned Lou and brought her up-to-date about the necklace test, Melanie's request for her help, and the threatening phone call. Lou was properly amazed that the necklace was not authentic, but, to Charlotte's dismay, was not much impressed with the threat.

"Just kids," she said, dismissing the call altogether. She was considerably more interested in how Charlotte was organizing her article research on the necklace.

"This photo McClanahan gave me is a place to start because it shows the people surrounding Phil when he said there was a fake," Charlotte said. "I remember when the picture was taken and it was right at that time. Of course, I don't consider these people suspects, really. But they did know that he said there was a fake. If one of them was the person who stole the real jade necklace from the show and slipped in the fake one, then maybe Melanie's right that someone had a motive for killing Phil. Or maybe their motive was not to cover up their theft but to simply protect the show. I have the feeling that a few careers may be riding on the success of this exhibit."

"You've simply got to stop reading those murder mysteries, Charlotte. They're affecting your mind."

"As I remember, that's what you said when I told you there was a fake in the Son of Heaven show," Charlotte retorted.

"I stand corrected," Lou said. "Forgive my demands for some kind of empirical evidence on which to base your opinions. Just some little bit of evidence . . . like a coroner's ruling of murder, for instance."

"I don't really think Phil was murdered, either," Charlotte had to say. "But since these people in the photo must have heard him make his allegations, I'll eventually have to in-

terview them for my necklace articles, anyway. Right now,
I'm just going to try to find out some preliminary information, including whether they have any connections with
Chinese art. And, for Melanie's sake, where they were the
night Phil died."

"Who's in the picture?" Lou asked.

McClanahan had attached the text that would have run
under the picture had it been published.

"There's Adam Walker—he's the tanned and silvery plastic surgeon, remember? His wife is there, too. Barry Abrams
and Libby Fox, of course, and Sigrid Olson."

"That's seven people, counting Phil and you. Phil's dead,
and I feel certain you—or anybody else—didn't kill him.
So that leaves five pseudo-suspects, Charlotte."

"You sound like you're selling seashells by the seashore."

"Regardless, five seems quite enough."

"I think so, too. Now I've got to figure out a way to get
these people to talk with me." Charlotte paused, considering, then said, "I think I'll skip Barry and Libby for the time
being."

"Why?"

"I'm going to assume they were where they said they were
when Phil died. Frankly, I find Libby about the most un-
suspicious person you could imagine. Maybe I just like her
and that's my only reason for not suspecting her."

Lou pointed out that her reasoning wasn't particularly
objective.

"I don't feel that way about Barry," Charlotte went on,
"but he told me he was working in his office at Central that
night. I think that if he was making up an alibi, he would
have made up one that put him miles from the scene of the
crime."

"That sounds more logical," said Lou the psychologist.
"You *do* use an interesting combination of right- and left-
brain thinking, Charlotte."

"I wish you'd stop analyzing my thinking and help me
figure out what to do."

"You're pacing around your office right now, aren't you? I can always tell."

Charlotte groaned and sat down at her desk.

"Why don't you just interview the people in your picture for your articles on the necklace now instead of eventually?" Lou suggested.

"I can't even *mention* an article because of my promise to Libby. I'll just have to poke around and try to figure out what I can."

"That would let you make good on your promise to ask some questions for Melanie."

"Right," agreed Charlotte, adding to herself that it would also let her investigate whether any of the people she talked with could have made the metallic-voiced phone threat. Or maybe she'd find out they had received phone threats, too, she realized for the first time.

"Are you still there, Charlotte?"

"What?"

"I was just saying that I have a suggestion about how you can get these people in the photo to talk with you." Lou paused, and then said, "I believe all your psuedo-suspects except Libby and Barry are sponsors or representatives of corporate sponsors of Son of Heaven. Am I right? What if you told them you're doing a pilot survey for the Institute for Research on Career Development?"

"IRCD? Where you used to work?"

"Certainly. The survey could be about something like, oh, the sponsors' perceptions of the effect of sponsorship on their career development. And while you're getting their opinions about that, it will probably just naturally come up that this poor Oriental art history expert died at the Son of Heaven exhibit and what did they think about that, and they'll probably respond with what they were doing that night. Or they'll bring up the scene Phil made at the Son of Heaven affair. If they don't, you can nudge them a little. If they don't have anything to hide, they'll be perfectly willing to talk."

By this time, Lou could tell Charlotte had started pacing again.

"Of course," Lou went on, "the guilty one isn't likely to break down and confess, but at least you can find out who acts funny about the necklace. *And* who doesn't have an alibi for the evening Phil died."

"Well, unless someone was home with *you,* you don't have an alibi for that evening, either," Charlotte pointed out.

"If what you're trying to say is that innocent people don't always have alibis, I'm afraid you're right. However, if the police checked me out, they'd find a phone call from my phone number to my niece in New Jersey. She's getting married next month, so we were discussing her bridal shower."

Charlotte considered Lou's research-project idea. "If your old boss finds out I've involved IRCD's good name, I won't have to worry about telephone threats," she said. "Dr. P. B. Newman will kill me himself."

"On the other hand, this is clearly a case where it's easier to get forgiveness than permission," Lou told her. "And you really need a research cover so you can ask impertinent questions of your suspects."

Later that day, Charlotte reviewed her list of suspects before calling each of them for an appointment. She toyed with the idea of adding her cousin Melanie to the list.

It was very difficult to imagine the passive Melanie striking anyone, let alone killing her own husband. On the other hand, Charlotte felt certain that if by some wild quirk of fate *she* had married Phil Stevenson, she would have had to kill him—or herself—quite apart from any fake necklace.

Wednesday

The next day, Charlotte phoned Lou to report that the only time Dr. Adam Walker could talk with her conflicted with the time she had scheduled an appointment with his wife Daphne.

"Why aren't you going to interview them together?" asked Lou.

"If I talk to them at the same time, they'll just confirm each other's statements," Charlotte explained. "I'd like to call Daphne back and tell her 'my colleague' Lou Toreson will be interviewing her instead. Can I do that?"

"What is this? I get to be the one to go talk with a forty-year-old debutante? Charlotte, you've assigned me the kind of person I appreciate least."

"Come on. You can talk to her about how you're a volunteer at Son of Heaven. I bet she'd be more receptive to an interview with you than with me, anyway."

"Flattery will not work with me, Charlotte."

"How about guilt? Just think of all the times you've gotten *me* into things. Remember the sensory-deprivation experiment? That was a good one. In fact, now that I think about it, it was you who insisted we go to the Son of Heaven gala where all this got started. You owe me, Lou."

"Stop pacing," Lou said. But Charlotte knew her friend had already agreed.

15

Thursday

Charlotte parked behind the blue BMW with the SIGRID vanity license plate. She was across the street from Schiller Park and in front of Sigrid Olson's story-and-a-half restored brick house in the German Village section of Columbus, directly south of downtown.

When Charlotte had called to set up the interview, Sigrid had told her firmly that the only possible time they could talk would be during Sigrid's noon workout. Charlotte's assumption that the working out would take place at one of the downtown athletic clubs near Sigrid's office, or even at the less chic YWCA, was proved false when Sigrid gave her the address on Jaeger Street.

For more than thirty years, the powerful German Village Association had masterminded the restoration of the area's rundown, but still sound, brick homes, duplexes, and defunct breweries. During the last ten years, German Village had turned into an enclave for yuppies like Sigrid.

As Charlotte used the brass door knocker, shaped like a buckeye, on Sigrid's front door, she questioned whether the decor met German Village Association standards for restoration: the stained-glass panel on one side of the door showed the OSU "block O" emblem; the one on the other side was of a blond female basketball player dunking the ball.

After a few moments, the door was opened by a sweating Sigrid. She was mopping her face with an electric-blue towel that matched the electric-blue Spandex bicycle shorts and top she was wearing, which, of course, matched her electric-blue eyes. She was obviously conscientious about staying in shape, Charlotte saw; there were no extra ounces on Sigrid's shapely six-foot frame. No doubt she met the village association's standards, Charlotte thought.

"Come in," Sigrid panted. "I'm in the middle of my program, but we can talk while I work."

Charlotte was amused to see that most of the first floor of the house had been converted into one large room and that most of that room was filled with chrome-coated steel exercise equipment. There was a small kitchen area in the back and a circular stair leading to a loft bedroom. A closed door at the back was probably the bathroom. Or maybe a tanning booth, Charlotte thought, judging by the color of Sigrid's skin not encased in Spandex. The sheer curtains were closed, so the large exercise area was in semidarkness. Charlotte could hear soft classical music playing in the background and was surprised that it was not the oppressive, driving music that she thought Sigrid would have been more likely to listen to.

The athlete got into position on the rowing machine. "What was it that you wanted to ask me about? Our CP and L sponsorship of the Son of Heaven exhibit?" she said between strokes.

Charlotte explained briefly and then took out her list and asked the first few questions about any effect Sigrid expected her company's sponsorship would have on her own career development.

Sigrid responded rather jerkily that it could only help; but Charlotte marveled that she could speak at all while rowing so strenuously. However, when Charlotte asked, "Did you hear about the death of Capital's Oriental art history expert at the Son of Heaven exhibit?" Sigrid stopped rowing abruptly, stared at Charlotte a moment, then resumed her exercise.

"Yes, I know Phil died," she said. "It makes me really angry. He had been so nice to me at the Son of Heaven meetings."

Astonished, Charlotte blurted out, "But he seemed to be such an obnoxious man."

"Not to me. It was nice to be around another athlete, someone who understood about training and practicing and trying your best to win. To depend on what you could do, not on whom you knew."

"I remember reading he was a wrestler in college," Charlotte said, but Sigrid seemed not to hear.

"He helped me with CP and L's Son of Heaven sponsorship," she went on. "It's so important that this come off well for me because it's my first really big project." She spoke so fiercely that Charlotte was taken aback, and she couldn't decide whether Sigrid was actually responding to her questions concerning career development or reminiscing about Phil.

Sigrid went on. "I didn't talk with him that evening at the dinner, but I heard him say all that stuff about there being a fake. And then he was dead."

Suddenly, Sigrid looked up at Charlotte and announced that she had to get through the last three parts of her routine in fifteen minutes, so Charlotte would have to leave. "We can finish your interview in my office next week. I'll have my secretary call you to set a time," she said.

There didn't seem to be any way to keep Sigrid talking now—she was rowing more frantically than ever—so Charlotte agreed to put off the interview. She was keenly aware that she had not yet found out where Sigrid had been the night Phil died. Hoping that the atmosphere next time would be a little less kinetic, she determined she would make a point of finding out exactly how personal Phil and Sigrid's relationship had been.

There wasn't time for Charlotte to return to her office before her downtown appointment with Adam Walker at two-thirty. So she drove north to the capitol and parked in the underground parking garage. She walked over to Lazarus to pick up a shirt for Ty and a new purse for herself. As long as she was there, it seemed only smart to browse the second-floor jewelry department to decide whether it was time to steer Walt that way the next time they were in the store. Some peridot earrings caught her eye.

Adam Walker mentioned the lapis earrings she was wearing during their conversation at the Broad Street Club later that afternoon. It was one of several charming things he did that seemed intended to make her feel comfortable in their rather imposing surroundings.

Charlotte had never been in this club before, having turned down previous dining invitations because women were not permitted as members. But this time, she had been so interested in interviewing Walker that she had agreed to meet there for a drink. Unfortunately, ever since she had walked in the front door, she had felt like a traitor and already knew full well she wouldn't tell Walt or Lou where she had met Walker.

She had expected the decor to be relentlessly male—dark colors, lots of wood, and heavy furniture—but was pleasantly surprised to find pastel colors used extensively. She was escorted through several rooms to join Adam in a bright sunny room filled with green plants, comfortable chairs, and glass-topped tables.

One wall and part of the ceiling were glass. She hadn't been aware that it was such a sunny day before coming into the club. Perhaps the wealthy club members could import their own sunlight, she thought. Or, more likely, she realized, every available sun ray brought in through the glass bounced off so many reflective surfaces within the room that its light was enhanced. The effect was dazzling.

Adam stood to greet her. He was dazzling, too: tall, with a narrow, youthful-looking face and even features, and that silvery hair she remembered from the exhibit affair. His pale-blue eyes were all the more noticeable against his dark tan but were just a tad on the cool side to suit Charlotte's taste. Charlotte would have been willing to bet the tan was from the beach at Bimini rather than from one of the local tanning parlors. She was curious about why a physician would risk skin cancer, but he sure looked good.

"How good of you to meet me here, Charlotte," Adam said as she was seated. "I'm due at Grant Hospital in an hour, and this seemed the nicest spot to get together. I hope I didn't take you too far out of your way."

Lying through her teeth, Charlotte assured him that she had not been troubled by the location. Then she brought out her list of interview questions and thanked him for agreeing to help with her research. He caught her by surprise by saying, "This is a little different for you, isn't it? Doing survey research, I mean. I've read your articles, but I don't remember anything like this."

The jig is up, she thought, for once sorry that someone recognized her work. She forced herself to reply calmly.

"It's nice to know somebody out there is reading my articles."

"With great interest," Adam said, smiling.

Charlotte found herself instantly concocting a justification for the interview. "Actually, I'm less interested in survey research than I am in career development," she said, hoping that her years of conversations with Lou about career development had prepared her to make it sound believable.

"The survey just seemed the most reasonable way to collect this particular information," she said. "After this first article I plan a whole series about career development. I'm very interested in finding out how people chose their careers, the factors that influence their choice, and how their careers progress."

Adam seemed satisfied, not suspicious, so she asked the first survey question. From then on it was smooth sailing. Adam seemed anxious to impress Charlotte, and he succeeded. He was intelligent, although somewhat humorless, and quite attentive.

At first she found herself concentrating as much on his physical appearance as on what he was saying. She took notes only on what he said, but mentally noted his large gold cuff links, the brilliance of his white shirt, and the absence of wrinkles on his face and neck. But by the middle of the interview, she had regained enough of her usual cynicism to begin to notice small imperfections in the doctor, such as his smaller-than-average hands. Maybe, she thought, their size was an advantage in surgery as he made precise nips and tucks in his grateful patients.

There were no rings on his fingers, and Charlotte wondered whether that had something to do with always having to scrub for surgery. Daphne, she mentally advised his wife, if he were mine, I'd make sure he wore a wedding band.

Adam told her that he sponsored cultural activities such as the Son of Heaven because he wanted to give something back to a community that had been so good to him. Charlotte considered his answer to be pretty standard pap—harmless but dull. Had this been a legitimate interview, she would have pressed him for something more revealing. But since it wasn't, she asked her other innocuous questions and eventually steered the interview toward Phil Stevenson's scene at the gala.

She asked Adam whether had had heard Phil's outburst. He said he had heard "some drunken, incoherent ramblings that I couldn't make sense of," and thought it was a damn shame that someone like that would try to ruin a show that so many people had worked so hard on.

Pap, pap, pap, Charlotte thought.

He was more specific in telling her that he had been catching up on case notes in his Riverside Medical Building office all evening the night Phil died. She probed somewhat obliquely at whether he had ever been threatened or otherwise felt endangered as the result of his cultural activities. But Adam got the point of her question.

"No," he said, "unless you count the damage to my gastrointestinal system from all the bad dinners," he said heartily.

While Charlotte spent a pleasant hour with Dr. Walker, Lou was on her way to her interview with Daphne Walker. The Walkers' condominium apartment was on the northeast corner of the Waterford Tower, a new downtown high-rise whose high-tech security arrangements were rumored to be the strongest in the city. A maid admitted Lou into the Walkers' foyer, which was hung with expensive-looking art. None of it looked Chinese, Lou noted so she could tell Charlotte later. The maid escorted her into the Walker's living-dining room.

It was too cold to go out on the huge balcony that extended from the northeast corner of the room, but Lou could imagine how nice it would be in the summer. When Daphne joined her, Lou was gazing out the windows at the Scioto River, the Broad Street Bridge, and Columbus Central, noting that Daphne could easily walk to the Son of Heaven show.

Lou accepted Daphne's offer of tea, and soon they were seated in uncomfortable straight-backed chairs that reminded Lou of furniture designed by Frank Lloyd Wright. Lou munched a cookie, but Daphne was having only tea. Abstinence and exercise may have produced Daphne's slim figure, but Lou was virtually certain that the smooth face had been produced by her husband or one of his colleagues.

In response to a question, Daphne explained that the Walkers' interest in art dated back to their first meeting. She had met Adam at a members' reception for the opening of a traveling exhibit at the Columbus Museum of Art. She couldn't remember who the artist had been—it had been over twenty years ago—some photographer, she believed.

Further questions from Lou uncovered that, although Adam was on the museum board, Daphne had made the decision to help sponsor Son of Heaven. Because Charlotte had insisted that Lou try to find out whether Daphne had received a telephone threat, Lou dutifully asked whether

Daphne had ever found herself endangered by her cultural activities.

"What an odd question," Daphne said. "Whatever do you mean?"

"I was wondering whether the public ever bothered you or your husband, once people read about your sponsorships, for instance. Are you pestered by people trying to get you to donate money to them personally? Has anyone ever threatened you when you turned down their request that you sponsor an affair?"

"Of course not," Daphne said. "We wouldn't deal with that kind of person. I don't know how you could think of such a thing."

"Of course," said Lou.

Most of Daphne's activities, it seemed, were centered around art. Art was her first love, she said. After all, art stayed where you put it—unlike children, for example.

"Speaking of children," said Lou. "I noticed in the paper that the Oriental art history expert who died over at Son of Heaven last week had three children."

"Yes, wasn't that awful about him dying. And such terrible weather that night."

Lou agreed with both sentiments, but had the odd feeling that Daphne considered Phil's death and the bad weather to be of equal consequence.

Daphne reached over to the antique table next to her chair and picked up the largest Filofax binder Lou had ever seen. The cover was some exotic-looking gray skin that Lou imagined had originated in the ocean depths. Daphne quickly flipped open the binder, read from it a moment, and raised her eyes to Lou.

"That's what I thought," she said. "I had taken the Mercedes over to the underground garage at Capitol Square to go to the Chamber of Commerce meeting that evening."

If everyone so quickly volunteers their whereabouts, Lou thought, Charlotte will have her murderer before a jury the day after tomorrow.

Daphne continued. "That way, I could just walk through the tunnel under High Street into the building where the meeting was held."

Lou was watching for signs of nervousness, but Daphne remained calm. "The meeting just went on and on—we didn't leave until midnight. Once I saw the ice, I accepted my neighbor's offer of a ride home and I left the Mercedes there under the capitol overnight."

"Was Dr. Walker at the meeting with you?" Lou asked casually.

"No," Daphne answered. "I represented both of us as Son of Heaven sponsors." From a folder in the Filofax, she took out the minutes of the meeting, which listed those in attendance, and handed the sheet to Lou.

"Adam took the Lamborghini to his office to catch up on case notes," Daphne said. "As it turned out, he was able to get home before I did."

Lou had the information Charlotte needed: Daphne's name was on the list, but not her husband's. After asking a few cursory questions about the impact the Son of Heaven exhibit was likely to have on Daphne's "career" as an art collector, Lou drew the interview to a close, thanked the woman for her help, and left.

Late in the day she phoned Charlotte to describe the interview in detail but cut it short because Charlotte sounded so tired.

"Basically, I don't think Daphne is your necklace thief, Charlotte," she summarized. "The Walkers seem to be loaded, and she can prove she was at a Chamber of Commerce meeting the night Phil died. I saw the minutes of the meeting, and she was listed among those who attended."

"You saw the minutes?"

"Let's just say this woman is well organized," Lou said. "But her husband wasn't with her at the meeting. She said he was at his office, writing up case notes. Is that what he told you?"

"Yep. And he didn't seem the least bit suspicious, either."

"You sound terrible, Charlotte. Why don't you get some rest this weekend?"

"Maybe I'll be able to. All we have planned is Phil's memorial service on Sunday. How's that for an exciting social life?"

"It's symptomatic of your attitude about this necklace business. You've been a little obsessed with it all, you know."

"I'm getting the same complaint from my husband. But Ty thinks it's interesting. Last night he taped an outline of a person on the floor of his bedroom. It looks like the chalk outline the police make around the body of a murder victim."

16

Charlotte entered her office with hopes for a day of uninterrupted work on the Ohio Penitentiary article. But her attention was immediately caught by a package, wrapped in brown paper, sitting on her desk. According to a note in Claudia's neat handwriting, the package had been outside the office door when Claudia arrived at eight-thirty. Claudia was now off to the library, the note continued, and would see Charlotte after lunch.

She picked up the package and turned it over. It looked to be about nine inches on a side. There was no return address or postmark on it, and Charlotte's name and office address were typed on a label that had no other identifying marks.

She didn't have a clue as to who had sent it. Perhaps it was from Walt, that romantic devil. Perhaps not, given that Walter's gifts were never a mystery, as he required full credit for his generosity.

How nice to get a present from *someone*, Charlotte thought. As she opened the outer wrappings of the package, she noticed how carefully it had been taped. Inside were two layers of those plastic bubbles Ty loved to pop, which she put aside for him. Whatever was inside must be fragile.

Underneath the bubbles were individually wrapped objects about the size of pillboxes. She carefully opened the first one. Inside was a piece of painted and glazed ceramic crockery. It was white, with bits of red, black, and green paint. The piece was intact, but it appeared to be a leg broken off a ceramic figurine.

How weird. Who would send her a broken leg? And why?

She unwrapped the next object and found it to be an arm broken off what looked like the same figurine. One by one she unwrapped the rest of the objects, growing increasingly apprehensive. They all turned out to be individual body parts of the same figurine. None of them was smashed, just unattached. The painted face looked Chinese, and it was definitely female. Assembling them loosely on her desk, Charlotte found that the pieces composed a seated woman wearing a flowing white robe or toga that had a hood.

She picked up the brown paper and the cardboard box the pieces had arrived in and searched frantically through them for a message—something that would explain what the broken figurine meant and why it had been sent to her.

There wasn't a clue. She was forced to consider that the message lay before her in the broken pieces. Someone had gone to a lot of trouble to send her a disassembled woman, and it was hard to miss the point. This woman had had more than her nose chopped off. Charlotte feared it was an escalation of the threat made to her over the phone. What would be next?

Someone was trying to scare her, which made her angry. It made her even angrier that he or she was succeeding.

Decisively, she called Lou and asked her for the name of the police detective who had been there when she identified Phil Stevenson's body.

"Got another body, Charlotte?"

"Sort of. A package arrived at my office this morning and it contains a broken figurine of a Chinese woman."

"I know those delivery people have no sense of responsibility whatsoever, but I've never thought of calling the police on them," Lou chuckled.

"Me either. I'm calling the police because I think this package was sent to scare me off the necklace investigation."

"Well, the detective's name is Barnes. Jefferson Barnes. But I think you're overreacting to the figurine. Somebody probably just dropped it."

"You don't understand, Lou. It didn't get smashed in the mail. The pieces were individually wrapped."

"Interesting. You said it looked Chinese?"

"Yes. That cheap-looking Chinese ceramic that you see in gift shops. It's all painted shiny white but there are some other colors, too. The figure is of a woman who is sitting down, and she's wearing a loose robe with a hood."

"Sounds like Kuan Yin to me," Lou said.

"How could you possibly have any idea who it is?"

"You consistently underestimate the Son of Heaven volunteer, Charlotte. They sell lots of Buddhist statues at the Son of Heaven gift shop, along with the other trinkets. I see them all the time. Tell me, does she have a kind of surprised look on her face?"

"Yes."

"That's Kuan Yin, all right. She sells for six ninety-five and was considered by the Chinese to be the protector of children."

"You're amazing. It's really creepy that this thing has a Son of Heaven connection. And now I'm *certain* I'm calling the cops."

After going through the Detective Bureau Main Desk operator, Charlotte's call reached Jefferson Barnes.

"Detective Barnes, my name is Charlotte Sams. I'm a cousin of Melanie Stevenson, the wife of the art history professor whose body was found at Columbus Central last week."

"Yes?"

"I wonder if I could come downtown and talk to you for a few minutes."

"What about?"

"Well," said Charlotte, "there's been nothing in the paper or on TV about Phil Stevenson's death since last Wednesday. I wondered if we could talk about what happened."

"Look, lady," Barnes snapped. "I'm busy with lots of cases

in the southwest quadrant right now. I don't have time for chitchat."

Since everything else in the city seemed to be measured from the intersection of Broad and High streets, Charlotte assumed that the quadrant Barnes referred to was the area south of Broad Street (the major east-west street through the city) and west of High Street (ditto for north-south). Columbus Central was on the south side of Broad Street and about four blocks west of High Street, across the Scioto River.

She tried again. "Detective Barnes, someone threatened me a few nights ago. Over the phone. And then this morning someone sent me a threat. I think this is connected with Phil Stevenson's accusation that there is a fake in the show, maybe even connected with his death, and I'd really like to talk to you about it."

Barnes was quiet a moment, then said, "Can you come down here around one o'clock?"

"Yes. Thank you," Charlotte said. "I'll be there at one."

"I'll give your name—Sams, right?—to the duty officer on the first floor. Just tell him you're here to talk to me." Barnes hung up.

Later, as she drove downtown to see Barnes, Charlotte's thoughts turned to Barry Abrams and Libby Fox. Should she tell them about the threatening call and the broken figurine? Since they, too, knew about the fake necklace, they might also be in danger. Or maybe one or both of them were responsible for the call and the figurine. The voice on the phone had been so disguised that she couldn't even be sure whether it had been a man or a woman. Would the manager of an art show or the sponsoring museum's director be willing to threaten people to make the show a success?

Neither of the Walkers seemed to be likely suspects, based on the information she and Lou had gotten in their interviews. But Sigrid was a different story. She had seemed so fierce about the importance of Son of Heaven to her career.

What if she had considered Phil's announcement of a fake as a threat to sabotage the show?

Charlotte parked at a one-hour meter on Marconi, got out, and had to dig to the bottom of her purse to find coins after discovering her change purse was empty. She pulled things out of her purse and onto the hood of the car. Billfold, lipstick, comb, old charge slips, tissues, notebook, pens, pencils, the photo of her pseudo-suspects, a bag of orthodontic elastics for Tyler's braces. At last, some coins.

As she put the other stuff back in her purse and put the money in the meter, she reflected that mothers could trace the growth of their children by the items they carried in their purses. Hers used to be full of little round-headed Fisher-Price "people." Then came the Matchbox cars. Now it was elastics for braces. What would she be carrying for him next year, when Ty began his teenage years?

She walked down the street to the city's main police station. According to the cornerstone, it had been built in 1929, just before the stock market crash. No wonder it was scheduled for replacement in a couple of years.

She found the duty officer in his block-and-glass cage just inside the first-floor entrance and told him that she had an appointment with Detective Barnes. He phoned up to the third floor and soon Barnes was there to take her up to the open area behind locked doors—filled with desks, computers, and file cabinets—that was the space where downtown Columbus detectives worked. This was Charlotte's first time here, and she was relieved to be leaving the area where criminals entered before being booked.

They moved to Barnes's desk, where he sat down on a swivel chair while Charlotte took a straight wooden chair. There were a couple of other men in the room, both using the phone. She quickly took a moment to assess Barnes. Lou had not mentioned that he was such a large man. He was barrel-chested, with large facial features and a trim mustache that looked too small for his face. His red tie was loose at the neck, and he unbuttoned his sport jacket as he swiveled in his chair toward Charlotte and said, "So. Tell me about the threats and why you think they are related to Phil Stevenson."

Charlotte told her story, carefully leaving out the part about her having verified Phil's fake with Armstrong's test. She wasn't willing yet to jeopardize the exclusivity of her articles; and, besides, there was her promise to Libby. Barnes already knew that Phil had claimed there was a fake, anyway, because Lou had told him so when she had identified Phil's body.

After she'd finished, Barnes said, "So you think someone wants to scare you or hurt you because you heard Stevenson say that Son of Heaven exhibit contains a fake?"

"Yes."

"Then why isn't everybody who heard him being threatened?"

"Maybe because I'm a relative of Phil's and whoever is doing this thinks I'd take his last accusations more seriously than other people would."

"Would you?"

"What?"

"Would you take his accusations more seriously?"

"I don't know. Phil and I didn't get along very well and—" Charlotte stopped abruptly when she realized that information could sound incriminating. "No one got along very well with Phil," she ended lamely.

"I've gotten the feeling he didn't have a very big fan club," Barnes said. "You have any particular reason not to like him?"

"No." She couldn't resist adding, "Just the same reasons everybody else had."

"Did he tell you anything about his so-called fake after the Son of Heaven dinner on Sunday?"

"No. He wouldn't have had any reason to talk to me about it. Why are you asking?"

Barnes ignored Charlotte's question. "Perhaps you know someone else that he would have wanted to examine the piece he suspected?"

"Of course not," she said. "I don't really know much about art or art experts in town."

"Do you know anyone that Stevenson was likely to have met with Monday night? That would have been the night after that fancy dinner you all attended."

"No."

"Did you see Dr. Stevenson at all on Monday?"

"No."

"Did you talk with him at all between the dinner and the time his body was found?"

"Why are you asking me all these questions?"

"Were you at Central during that time?"

"Why would I have gone back to Central? I get the feeling you think *I* murdered Phil Stevenson," Charlotte said indignantly.

Barnes shifted in his chair and looked at Charlotte for a long moment. Finally, he said, "I don't think anybody murdered Stevenson, Ms. Sams. But you do. And I'm curious about why."

Charlotte remained silent. As she waited, Barnes's face lost some of it intensity, and she thought he looked a little weary as he continued, "Look, Ms. Sams. Our pathologists know that Stevenson died of a heart attack between eight and ten the night before his body was found. Fake or no, there's just no reason to think he was murdered."

"But aren't there ways to make it look like someone had a heart attack? Or ways to make a person actually have one?" Charlotte persisted, forgetting to act surprised at the information about the cause of death, which Melanie had already supplied her.

Barnes didn't seem to notice. "That's movie stuff," he said.

The room was quiet as they stared at one another.

"So you're not going to protect me?" Charlotte finally said.

"I don't think you *need* protecting, Ms. Sams. That phone call sounds like some kids playing a prank. You'd be surprised at the sophisticated electronic equipment some of these teenagers can hook up to disguise their voices."

"But think about what the voice said," Charlotte insisted. "That I'd get my nose cut off if I poked it in someplace where it didn't belong. That's a pretty old-fashioned phrase, poking your nose in where it doesn't belong. I don't think kids today are likely to use it."

"Frankly, it's a lot cleaner than what they are apt to say. Consider yourself lucky."

Charlotte again mentioned the broken figurine.

"A friend of yours sent you a gift that got broken in delivery," was Barnes's explanation.

"Nobody I know has bad enough taste to have bought that figurine," Charlotte said, exasperated. "Besides, as I told you, the unattached pieces were individually wrapped. The figurine was broken *before* it was sent to me."

"I'm sorry. I just can't work up much enthusiasm about a broken figurine. If you get another phone call, I suggest you call the phone company and change your number. They can do some traces, too. I'm afraid there's not much I can do for you."

"I still think it's too great a coincidence that an art history expert says there's a fake in an exhibit, the man turns up dead two days later, and threats are made to people who heard his accusations about the fake."

"None of the other people who have heard his accusations has been threatened," Barnes said testily.

"To your knowledge."

"To my knowledge."

"Well, maybe you should check with those other people and see if they've had any threatening experiences like mine," Charlotte suggested. She took the photograph of the psuedo-suspects out of her purse.

"I got this from the *Dispatch*," she said. "It was shot about the same time Phil was yelling about a fake, so all the people pictured heard him. Now you know who to ask about whether they've been threatened."

A silent Barnes took the photo out of her hands and studied it. Finally he looked up at her and said, "Ms. Sams, what do you do for a living?"

"I'm a writer."

"Well, why don't you go write and let professional police officers take care of protecting the public."

He stood up to hurry her on her way, but Charlotte got in a parting shot.

"You professionals didn't do such a hot job of protecting Phil Stevenson, did you?"

Unperturbed, Barnes said, "I'll keep your picture for a while."

Walking up Marconi to reclaim her car, Charlotte was furious with the patronizing Barnes.

Although he had kept the photo, it was obvious Barnes hadn't recognized a good idea when it was literally handed to him. She thought the police got paid for coming up with their own ideas. What kind of a job were they doing if they had to depend on citizens coming in—practically off the street—to crack their cases for them? she fumed.

In the car, she replayed her conversation with Barnes. She did not think he seriously considered her a suspect—especially since he maintained Phil was not murdered. But if that was true, why had he continued to question her about her contact with Phil after the exhibition dinner?

She got out her notebook from her purse and began writing down as many of his questions as she could remember. He had wanted to know whether she had talked with Phil between the time he had left the dinner and when his body was found. Or if she had met with him during that time. He had also asked if she had been back to Central then. He had asked, too, whether she knew anyone Phil would have wanted to examine the fake he had mentioned. Any art experts, he had suggested.

These didn't sound like the questions of a detective who thought the deceased had died of natural causes, she reflected. Why would he have wanted to know whether she had returned to Central? How come he wasn't trying to find out why *Phil* was there the night he died, instead of trying to connect her movements with Central? Then she realized, maybe he was. Many of his questions seemed to involve

Central. Maybe that was because he thought Phil had been there to meet with somebody—her or somebody who could really evaluate the necklace. Now that she thought about it, what other logical explanation could there be for those kinds of questions?

But if he really thought Phil was murdered, why wasn't he interested in protecting her? She hoped she wouldn't have to die to find out.

Sunday

C harlotte and Walt stood on the front lawn of Christ Lutheran Church. The big stone church was on East Main Street, right across from the Capital University campus.

They and Tyler had sat at the front of the church, behind the pew where Melanie and the children sat, listening to the "remembrance" eulogies for Phil Stevenson and singing along with the hymns. Now they were watching the other people who had attended the memorial service come out into the sunshine while Tyler talked with Melanie's older daughter, Chrys, as she stood by her mother right outside the door of the church.

None of the rest of Melanie's family had come to the service, nor were any of Phil's family in attendance. Perhaps they had gone to the funeral held the previous Thursday in Phil's Pennsylvania hometown.

The church, with its stained-glass windows and rows and rows of wooden pews, had not been filled, but there had been a good turnout. Phil's faculty colleagues and their wives had sat in a group toward the front on the left. His department chairman had delivered one of the remembrances, stressing Phil's brilliance as a scholar. Mrs. Marchand, the department secretary, spoke briefly and gently about missing Dr. Stevenson in the department.

Phil's contributions to the Son of Heaven organizational

"Wait till you hear *this*, Mom," Tyler said into the phone. It was his usual home-from-school call to check in with Charlotte. "You won't believe it."

"You got an A on a math test."

"Very funny," he said. "I've got something good to tell you, something to help you in your work, and you joke around."

"Sorry. Let's hear it."

"Well, you know my art class went down to the Son of Heaven today? While we were there, a kid put some gum on that big stone lion in the show."

"You're kidding! Which one?"

"The guide called it a chimera. It's that lion that sits in the hallway in front of the life-sized soldiers."

"No, I meant which kid," Charlotte said. "If that sculpture is the one I'm thinking of, it's over seventeen hundred years old."

"It was Benny Banks who did it. And boy, was the teacher mad."

"I'll bet."

"But the funniest part was that she bawled him out for just *touching* it. She didn't know that he had put gum on there and was rubbing it off."

"Did he get kicked out of the show?"

"No, but the tour guide made him walk with the teacher for the rest of the tour."

"I'm surprised she didn't kick him out. Lou says the guides have the authority to do that."

"Having to walk next to Mrs. Herndon would be punishment enough. I hate her."

"I assume you were on your best behavior?"

"No, Mom," he said in a pained, sarcastic tone. "I kicked over one of the vases."

She ignored it and suggested, "Maybe that kid—Benny—just *accidentally* touched the lion."

"Not a chance. It's behind a railing and he had to lean way over. Just a few of us saw what was going on."

"What did you think of the show?" she asked.

"It was okay. I liked the life-sized soldiers best."

Charlotte could have predicted that. She smiled to herself.

"I looked for that necklace you've been talking about, but I couldn't find it."

"I'm glad—it's supposed to be in the museum director's office. You didn't breathe a word about it to anybody, did you?"

"Thanks a lot," he said, insulted. "Sometimes you act like I'm a little kid."

"It's just that I don't want to take any chances about someone else finding out about the fake. Would I have told you about it if I thought you couldn't keep a secret?"

"I think you told me about it just because you wanted to tell Dad, and I was in the same room. If you could have thought of some way to get me to leave, I would never have known."

Since he wasn't far from the truth, Charlotte changed the subject. "How is this information about the gum supposed to help my work?" she asked.

"Because of the security. You said that the man from the show claimed he had great security. But ol' Benny got in there with his gum and no alarms went off or anything."

"Maybe the alarms rang someplace else. They don't always ring in the exhibit rooms."

"Well, nobody came running in from the outside. Benny had plenty of time to stick on the gum, change his mind, and start rubbing it off."

"Nothing happened until your teacher saw him?"

"Don't call her my teacher. I keep telling you I only see her when we go on field trips, and then she's a drill sergeant. I hate her."

"But nothing happened until Mrs. Herndon saw him?"

"Right."

"Well, that *is* helpful." Charlotte considered that perhaps Barry Abrams exaggerated the effectiveness of his security. To Ty she said, "Thanks. You did good."

"Don't mention it," he said, sounding exactly like his father.

When Walt came home from work that evening, he asked whether there had been an accident on their street. A police car was parked two doors down. Charlotte wasn't much interested in any accident once she learned that Walt, like Tyler earlier, had exhibit-security information to share with her. She had asked her husband to find out what company had the electrical contract for the remodeling of Columbus Central so that she could inquire about the security systems they had installed. She wasn't sure she could get that kind of information, but it never hurt to ask. When it turned out that Bartolucci Electric had the contract, Walt did the asking, since his friend Don worked there.

They sat with drinks in the living room and Charlotte told him about the gum incident.

"Maybe all it means is that it's a lot harder to prevent damage to art than to prevent art theft," Walt said. "I don't think that kid would have been able to pick up the lion and waltz out the door with it."

"Maybe. But then, I don't know yet what you found out today."

"Well, Don was quite free with his information," Walt

began. "I told him that you've gotten very interested in this show—and exhibit design in general. But I really didn't get into the necklace-theft part."

"Walter Sams, soul of discretion."

"That's me." Walt smiled. "Anyway, much of what Don told me is pretty predictable. For instance, he mentioned the movement sensors in every room that you had heard about from Abrams. And he said that all of the pieces in Plexiglas cases sit on pressure-sensitive pads so that, if anyone moved one, an alarm would sound."

As her husband spoke, Charlotte jotted down notes on a pad.

"Don said there's a security guard in every room of the exhibit. They act as though they are simply exhibit visitors."

"Really?"

"Yes. He said they dress like visitors and look at the art like visitors, but if you hang around long enough, you'd pick them out because you'd see that they never leave the room and go on to the next part of the show. Since real visitors don't hang around for hours, they don't detect the guards. Most of them wear those rented audiotape sets as part of their disguise."

"Sounds like a good idea."

"I suppose so, as long as they don't really turn the tapes on. If the tapes are playing, I bet anybody could grab the art and take off before the guard knew anything was wrong. You know how I worry about you wearing earphones on your walks."

"Let's not have another boring argument over earphones," Charlotte said. "Tell me what else Don said."

"Well, the most worrisome room, from a security standpoint, is the one that contains the Chime of Twenty-six Bells. That's because the bells aren't encased, just standing out there in the open."

The bronze bells, Charlotte knew, were from the mid-sixth century, when kneeling musicians struck them with wooden mallets during rituals and at court banquets.

"Why aren't they protected?" she asked.

"For the same reason that many paintings and other art works are not behind glass: it interferes with viewing the art. Don said that everything he and his designers came up with was considered by the museum staff to be either potentially damaging to the bell display or too intrusive. Finally, they just made sure that the bells were placed so no one could reach them without actually climbing a railing. And they also station extra security people in that room."

"Did Don's people do anything with the display forms like the one the jade necklace was in?"

"No. He said those were shipped intact from Seattle."

"I guess that means that the security for those cases was the same here as it was in Seattle."

"Sounds like it, doesn't it? One very interesting thing happened when the show was about ready to open. All the exhibits were in place, but then one of the museum staff noticed something wrong with the jade burial suit. Something about the placement of the suit inside its case."

Walt was referring to the second-century jade bodysuit in which a princess had been buried in the mistaken belief that it would keep her body from decaying. The suit was composed of more than two thousand 2-inch squares of pale-green jade that were tied together with gold thread strung through holes bored in the corners of each square.

"Did I mention that Don said the Plexiglas on the cases is exceptionally thick, much thicker than it looks? It looks—what?—maybe half an inch? Well, he said it's really at least an inch thick, and so strong that you couldn't break it with a hammer. Consequently, the Plexiglas on all the cases is very heavy."

"Maybe the weight of the glass is considered a security precaution in itself," Charlotte suggested.

"You might be right. All that Plexiglas over the jade burial suit weighs some eighteen hundred pounds."

"That's almost a ton!"

"Right. So the problem became how to lift the glass over the suit so that the suit could be rearranged."

"Why didn't they just rent some of your equipment? Don

knows that your mobile platforms could have lifted that glass easily."

"They were afraid to bring in any mechanized equipment at that point. It might have damaged the other displays that were all set up. Instead they rented some of those frames with suction cups on them that are used by glass companies to move big sheets of plate glass. They stationed twelve people around the perimeter of the burial-suit case. Each of them held one of those suction-cup frames. Then, on the count of three, they all used their frames to lift the glass about a foot and a half off the base of the display stand so a museum staff member could lean under there and adjust the suit."

"Each person would have had to lift more than a hundred pounds," Charlotte calculated.

"Don said that if the glass had slipped down onto the staff member leaning into the case, it would have cut him in two."

"Or her. Did he say who was brave enough to lean into that case?"

"No, he didn't. I got the feeling that he considers all the museum staff a little eccentric. Except for Libby Fox, of course. Don, like the rest of Columbus, seems to have succumbed to Libby's charms."

"I sure hope she doesn't turn out to be the necklace thief. I'm going to the library tomorrow to look at some old magazine and newspaper stories. Maybe I'll find out something that will implicate one of my other suspects."

Tyler joined them, flopping into an overstuffed chair and putting his stocking-covered feet on the coffee table.

"I've been meaning to ask you guys something," he said. "Do you ever go out after I'm in bed?"

"You mean, both of us at the same time?" Walt asked.

Tyler nodded yes.

"No," Walt said. "At least one of us is always here at night while you're sleeping."

"I thought you knew that," Charlotte said.

"That's what I thought, but I just thought I'd check."

"What brings this up?"

"Well, I was talking with Chrys yesterday and she told me that the night her dad died, she got up to get a drink and couldn't find her mom. She wasn't anywhere in the house. So I thought I'd make sure that you guys don't do that."

"Once you're in bed, one of us is always here, son," Walt said.

Yet another surprise from Melanie, Charlotte thought, worried about what she would learn next about her cousin.

19

Tuesday

Following her walk the next morning, Charlotte headed directly downtown to the main branch of the Columbus Metropolitan Library. It was always a pleasure to work in that ornate building, donated by Andrew Carnegie in 1904. The last library levy had provided funds to build a modern building, more than tripling the current space. But Charlotte was sorry that the old building would be used only for administrative purposes once the new one was completed.

Walking up the library's few front steps, she recalled the newspaper reports of last year's bitter budget meetings between the city and suburban libraries' directors. In one particularly acrimonious meeting, one director had punched another. With that one blow, the dueling director had probably done more to defeat the stereotype of passive, cerebral librarians than all their professional associations could hope to do in a lifetime.

She walked through the center hall on the first floor, a narrow, low-ceilinged passageway whose walls were covered with architects' renderings of what the new building would look like.

The hall emptied into the magazine, newspaper, and computerized-information service department. Throughout the room were long tables. On many of them were volumes of indexes, displayed spine out. Behind the librar-

ians' counter in the center of the room were several computer terminals for on-line searching of databases such as
ERIC, the national education database to which Lou had
introduced Charlotte.

She told a young librarian that she wanted to do some
research on current prominent Columbus residents. He led
the way to a nearby table and showed her how to use the
Columbus and Central Ohio News Index, contained in what
looked to be about twenty-five spiral-bound computer-
printout volumes.

This index, the librarian explained, contained citations
of articles in local publications since 1950, arranged by subjects referred to in the articles. The subjects, Charlotte was
happy to see, included names of persons. Each citation consisted of the headline that had appeared over the article
and the name, issue number or date, and page number of
the publication in which the article had appeared. Nine local
publications were indexed.

She started with the volume that contained citations for
the most recent articles, from January and February. One
by one, she plowed her way through all the volumes.

Within forty-five minutes, Charlotte had compiled a list
of citations of articles that referred to her suspects. The
articles were listed in chronological order.

Curious to see if she could find out more about Sigrid
and Phil's relationship, she decided to look first at the articles about Sigrid.

She took her list to the north end of the room and pulled
from the cabinets the rolls of microfilm containing the specific issues of publications she needed. Having seated herself
at one of the microfilm readers, she carefully threaded the
first roll into it. She flipped the switch and focused on the
front page of the April 7, 1977, *Columbus Dispatch* which
had appeared on the screen. Then she wound the film until
the screen was filled with that issue's sports pages.

She found the headline cited. It was over an article that
announced that Sigrid would attend Ohio State the next fall

on a basketball scholarship—one of the first the university had given to women basketball players. The article included the details of Sigrid's record performance at her high school in Youngstown and quoted the Ohio State women's basketball coach's praise and delight that Sigrid would henceforth play on the Lady Bucks' squad.

That was only the first of many articles that described Sigrid's prowess on the basketball court during the next four years, Charlotte discovered. Later articles announced the matriculated Sigrid's promotions at Columbus Power and Light. She joined the PR department in 1983 (having started with the utility company two years before), and became head of PR late in 1988. Sigrid was also the subject of a *Columbus Monthly* magazine personality profile shortly after her last promotion, about the time she started appearing in so many of the company's television commercials. There was a mention of her involvement with Son of Heaven, but no hint of any dealings with Stevenson.

Charlotte printed each article as soon as she had skimmed it, then inserted the microfilm containing articles about Adam Walker.

The earliest article appeared in May 1951, and featured Adam, a high school junior, because he had been selected by his teachers to attend music camp during the upcoming summer.

The article said that Adam wanted to be a doctor and that his after-school job was delivering the *Dispatch,* which probably accounted for such a long story being written about such an unremarkable fellow, Charlotte thought. It seemed to her that even now the *Dispatch* gave an unusual amount of space to its paper carriers.

In describing him, the article said Adam had a younger sister, Claire, that his father was a Methodist minister for a local church, and that the family lived on a street Charlotte knew to be in the blue-collar North Linden area of Columbus. So much for the teenaged Adam Walker.

Reading on, Charlotte learned that Daphne was Adam's

second wife. His father officiated at Adam's first wedding ceremony, when he married a Margot Carr of Bellefontaine, Ohio, in June 1956. The article said that the young couple had met at Ohio State University, where Adam had just completed his pre-med training and Margot her nursing degree. He was to begin medical school at Western Reserve University in Cleveland that fall, and Margot would be nursing at Cuyahoga County Community Hospital, also in Cleveland. The accompanying photo of the newlyweds showed that Walker was good-looking even then—before the tan and the silvey hair—and that Margot looked intelligent and friendly.

A 1964 article reported the Walker/Campbell family's donation of some fourteen hundred Chinese items to Ohio State University. Charlotte read that the parents of Adam's mother, Mary and George Otto Campbell, had been Methodist missionaries in China from 1889 to about 1900, at which time they were driven out by the Boxer Rebellion, bringing along the items now donated to OSU. Adam's mother, Sarah, had inherited them after her parents' death, and now the family was turning them over to the university "to be enjoyed by a wider audience."

At last a definite Chinese connection, Charlotte thought.

The article said that Adam and Margot had returned from Cleveland the year before, after Adam had completed his residency in cosmetic surgery at the Cleveland Clinic. Charlotte was interested to see that the photo accompanying this story included Adam, his sister, his parents, and a very pregnant Margot Walker. Adam looked about the same, but Margot looked considerably older than she did in her wedding picture. She smiled bravely over he protruding stomach, and the sentimental Charlotte was reminded of her own largeness at a similar time in her own life. Perhaps for that reason, she decided she liked Margot Walker.

A second wedding story detailed an event that put Columbus socialite Daphne Barnett in the bride's role on October 15, 1970. The ceremony had been held at St. Joseph's

Cathedral downtown and the reception at Scioto Country Club in wealthy suburban Upper Arlington. Daphne had been educated at Smith College. Judging from the size of the wedding, the play of the story, and the guests described, her parents were clearly well-connected in Columbus's social scene.

There was no mention of the Reverend Walker's having officiated at this wedding ceremony, and Charlotte wondered how Adam's Methodist parents had taken the announcement that their son would marry a Roman Catholic. It was at that point she realized that Margot Walker had to have died before Adam married Daphne. It was simply very unlikely that even so prominent a young woman as Daphne would have been permitted by the Church to marry a divorced man in a cathedral—or anywhere else, for that matter—in 1970.

The articles since 1970 that mentioned Adam mostly referred to his activities as a member of museum and symphony committees and other haunts of Columbus's elite. In 1980 he had been quoted in a *Columbus Monthly* article about cosmetic surgery. That was the sum total of the local printed record on Dr. Adam Walker.

One more suspect left to read about, given that Charlotte thought she knew enough about Libby Fox.

The material on Barry Abrams was familiar to her from conversations with Lou about Son of Heaven—with one exception. In a "People to Watch" blurb about him in the recent January *Columbus Monthly,* it was pointed out that Abrams had been arrested twice during the 1970s for public brawling in Washington, D.C., when he worked at a gallery specializing in Chinese art.

Feeling that she knew her suspects much better now, Charlotte placed the microfilm rolls on a table for staff reshelving and paid for the paper copies she had made. It was nearly time for her appointment with Richard Ransom, the art-insurance expert who had sat at her table at the Son of Heaven dinner.

Columbus's downtown contained the home offices of seventy-four insurance companies, including some major national insurers whose red marble buildings occupied whole city blocks. Alliance's building was not nearly as elaborate as those behemoths, befitting its shorter stature in the insurance world. Nonetheless, Charlotte thought, its art-deco atmosphere was impressive in a tasteful, less ostentatious way.

Once inside, she stopped to look at the collection of wall hangings and ceramics in the Alliance lobby. Her purpose had less to do with appreciating the work than with collecting her thoughts on how to approach Ransom to get the background information she needed for her articles without revealing the fake necklace.

On the eleventh floor, a secretary escorted Charlotte into Ransom's corner office. Ransom, looking fit and elegantly tailored, rose from behind his desk and shook Charlotte's hand. Each of them insisted first names be used. As Ransom conferred briefly with his secretary, Charlotte had a moment to look around. What was nicest about this office, she decided, was that everything was at eye-level: out the wide north and west windows of his office, one had a striking view of most of Columbus's major buildings. And on the walls opposite the windows, there was a collection of impressive paintings. Not a Chinese one in the bunch, she noted. Charlotte thought she recognized a Bellows among them, and moved closer to take a look at the signature. She was pleased to have her identification confirmed, and impressed at what Alliance was obviously wiling to pay for art to hang in its employees' offices. Bellows was Columbus's most prestigious artist and his works hung in museums around the world.

The secretary left, and Ransom asked Charlotte to join him at a comfortable sofa-and-coffee-table arrangement. She was glad to be seated away from the windows because she had a morbid fear of heights. Generally, it was high *open* spaces that scared her most, but like many people who feared heights, she grew weak in the knees when her vantage point was higher than standing on a chair.

When they were seated, Charlotte mentioned the paintings on his walls and asked Ransom if he had selected them.

"I own them," Ransom answered with obvious pride. "I'm afraid my employer has neither the will nor the taste to put together such a collection."

She was surprised at the vehemence with which he had made this last statemtent. Ransom was, too, perhaps, because he looked for a moment as though he regretted it. Then, laughing lightly in what Charlotte thought was an attempt to cover his discomfort, he quickly went on.

"I've built this collection over the last twenty years or so, beginning when I was in college."

"It's wonderful," Charlotte said admiringly.

"I have a few pieces at home, but it's much smarter to keep most of the collection here because the security in this building is so much stronger than what a private residence can reasonably offer. Unless you don't mind turning your home into an armed camp, of course."

Ransom leaned back on the sofa. "And then I also spend more of my waking hours here than I do at home," he said. "Eventually I decided that I'd get more enjoyment out of the collection if I kept it here."

"I suppose an insurance company building *is* one of the safest places around," Charlotte said, "assuming, of course, that you insurance folks actually put into practice the risk management you preach to the rest of us."

"That we do. Risk management is a topic on everyone's lips around here, as you would imagine."

He smiled and poured coffee for the two of them from a pot on the coffee table.

"I don't mean to sound patronizing," he said, handing Charlotte a steaming cup, "but I was surprised to hear you use the term 'risk management.' Most people don't know the meaning of that term. Although it refers to a simple concept, it doesn't seem to be a part of the average person's vocabulary."

"I suppose not," said Charlotte. "I'm sure I learned it because my husband and I own a small construction-related company to which insurance is crucial. We rent mobile platforms that lift workers and equipment as high as sixty feet in the air."

Ransom shook his head sympathetically. "I can just imagine your liability-insurance premiums," he commented.

"Right. But our company couldn't afford to operate even for one day without liability insurance. The equipment's quite reliable, but I'm afraid the workers aren't. They treat our mobile platforms pretty casually. They've even been known to drive them off loading docks. Our insurance carriers, of course, made us familiar with the term 'risk management' right off," she said.

"Did you want to talk about insuring your company's art with me?" Ransom asked.

"Oh no," Charlotte said. "I'm afraid I owe you an apology if I gave that impression when I called. I only wish I had some art worth insuring. Perhaps I will someday."

Ransom smiled tolerantly.

"No, I'm here to ask you for a favor," she continued. "I'm interested in writing about how works of art should be cared for. And properly insuring them is one aspect of that care."

Ransom nodded encouragingly. Charlotte paused and then plunged on. "I'm hoping you'd be willing to help my education along here by telling me a little about the art-insurance field."

She waited, trying to look earnest, hoping that Ransom would fall for what even to her own ears sounded like a pretty lame explanation.

Ransom asked, "What publication are you writing for?"

"Oh, I'm not far enough along yet to be targeting a particular magazine," Charlotte answered breezily, afraid that he would refuse to talk for fear of actually being quoted. "I've got a lot to learn yet before I get to that point. I'm really just trying to develop some background knowledge right now."

To her immense relief, Ransom smiled. "I'm almost always willing to talk about art," he said. "Matters relating to insuring works of art have become an avocation with me, which I suppose is just as well, since they have occupied so much of my business life."

Charlotte smiled and relaxed. He was going to do it.

"To give you a bit of history," Ransom went on, "let me say that the origins of fine-arts insurance lie in marine insurance, which is the oldest known form of insurance. Lloyd's of London had become the world's leading marine insurer by 1771, and that's still true today."

"I remember reading in the paper that it was Lloyd's that had insured the Columbus Museum's Ming bowl that was stolen in January," Charlotte said.

"That's right. Lloyd's insures the museum's permanent collection. We insure the loan collection."

"Does Alliance's corporate sponsorship of Son of Heaven mean that your company also has the insurance contracts for that show?"

"Not at all. I believe Lloyd's took all those contracts in a clean sweep. We're helping sponsor Son of Heaven out of a sense of civic pride. Or enlightened self-interest, if you will. When art does well in Columbus, then in the long run

Alliance Insurance does well, too." Here Ransom smiled again. "At least that's the pitch I made to our chairman of the board when I asked him to get the company involved."

"I have a friend who is a volunteer tour guide at Son of Heaven. She's heard that the show is insured for sixty-six million. Does that sound right to you?"

"I really couldn't say, since our company isn't one of the carriers."

"I didn't understand what you meant earlier when you said that fine-arts insurance is a part of marine insurance," Charlotte said. "How could paintings and sculpture require something that sounds like it comes from the sea?"

"Much insurance that covers broader risks than standard liability policies is lumped under the heading 'marine,' " he explained. "Specifically, it is *inland* marine insurance that's used to cover art works. Inland, as opposed to what's called 'wet' marine insurance."

"Is theft the major threat to art work?" Charlotte asked.

"Personally," he said, "I think the greatest threat is the physical deterioration that occurs naturally over time. The loss from deterioration is almost incalculable, and it's intensified by artists' use of inferior materials and, occasionally, by misguided restoration and preservation attempts. But if you're talking about threats that owners can insure against, then theft is the big one."

"Theft is certainly the one that gets the most attention in the media," Charlotte pointed out. "But I suppose that's because it's a lot more dramatic than natural deterioration, especially at today's prices."

"You're right about today's prices, but the most spectacular art thefts in history have generally been committed for reasons other than economics," Ransom said.

Charlotte was startled, never once having considered that the thief could have taken the jade necklace for any reason other than money.

"For centuries," Ransom continued, "art thieves stole art primarily for political or religious reasons. Members of a

society that had been victorious over another drew attention
to just how victorious they had been. They did that by stealing and displaying religious art works that were sacred to
those they had subdued."

Ransom then told Charlotte that in terms of dollar value,
art theft is believed to rank third, after narcotics and smug-
gling, on the world crime index. And that was just for the
thefts the police know about; many thefts, he said, go un-
reported.

Charlotte wanted to know why someone would not report
an art theft.

"For several reasons. For instance, it's embarrassing for
museums to admit art has been stolen from them. In addition, the directors and curators are sometimes afraid
they'll encourage copy-cat crime by providing publicity to
the thieves."

Charlotte had the feeling that her conversation with Ransom was winding down, so she told him how much she had
enjoyed their talk and appreciated his taking the time to
share so much information with her.

"I may be able to suggest another source of information
for you," Ransom said. "Not too long ago I had a similar
conversation with a local physician and art lover. He'd been
doing some reading about the brisk black market for art on
both U.S. coasts and had some wonderful stories to tell. He
mentioned a particular book that you might also find helpful. I'll jot down its name and author."

Charlotte soon left Ransom's office, but not before asking
him what "local physician and art lover" he had been referring to. He told her Adam Walker had recommended
the book and asked whether Charlotte knew the Walkers.

"I've met them," she managed to reply.

Driving home at the end of the day, Charlotte replayed
her conversation with Ransom in her mind. It was as she
was parking in front of her house, idly noticing the police
car parked again two doors down, that she was suddenly
brought up short. She realized Ransom had lied about Al-

iance's not having any of the insurance contracts for the Son of Heaven exhibit. She was certain because she distinctly remembered Libby Fox having said that she had looked at Alliance insurance documents once she had become suspicious of the necklace.

Now, why had Ransom done that? It was difficult to think of an innocent reason for the lie.

Damn, she thought. I'm not eliminating suspects; I'm gaining them.

21

Wednesday

Physicist Clayton Armstrong telephoned Charlotte at the office the next morning, right after she had hung up the phone from a conversation with saxophonist Conor Ennis, who had agreed to another meeting the following Friday. This was her last chance, because the article was due in the offices of *Ohio Blue Note* on the following Monday.

Armstrong apologized for taking so long to figure out the necklace's composition.

"We had to hunt a bit to find a signature that matched the necklace's," he told Charlotte. "It turns out the necklace is made of celluloid."

"Celluloid?"

"Yes. Celluloid was one of the first plastics. It's similar to Bakelite. Maybe you've seen old Bakelite jewelry and household items at flea markets?"

"Sure, but the necklace doesn't look like old Bakelite bracelets. It's beautiful. It looks like jade."

"I realize that. I'm just saying the two substances are chemically similar, Bakelite and celluloid."

"How old is the necklace?"

"Can't say. Celluloid was invented in 1869 but wasn't used much after the 1930s."

"Well, the necklace may be plastic, but it's still beautiful."

Armstrong agreed. Then Charlotte reminded the physicist of his pledge to keep the necklace replica a secret. After she hung up, she got ready for another visit with Sigrid, this one to be held in Sigrid's office.

After Sigrid apologized for her abrupt behavior the last time, she went on to explain to Charlotte how difficult it had been to convince CP&L to sponsor the Son of Heaven exhibit.

"That's why I was so upset when Phil said he'd found a fake in the show," Sigrid told her. "I believed him. He really did know everything about the history of Chinese art, so I was sure he wouldn't make up something like that. Art was the most important thing in the world to Phil."

"You seem to have known him pretty well," Charlotte probed, hoping, for Melanie's sake, that their relationship had not been personal.

"Oh, yes." Sigrid's response was bitter. "When we met at that first Son of Heaven meeting a couple of years ago, he was very flattering—you know the kind of thing—nice to meet another jock with brains *and* beauty, et cetera, et cetera." She shook her head at the memory.

"He pursued me until I believed he really did love me. We were together for about a year. And then he got careless and his wife found out about us and he dropped me flat.

"For the last six months I've tried to avoid him at meetings. Once I got over being hurt, all I wanted to do was smack him."

"Did you smack him?" asked Charlotte.

"Of course not," Sigrid snapped. "Oh, I get it. I bet you think he didn't have a heart attack. You think I killed him. Well, I didn't." She glared at Charlotte and stood up.

"Why would you think he was killed?" Charlotte said, trying to sound off-hand.

"Because he was always fooling around," Sigrid retorted. "Maybe his wife got tired of it."

She moved quickly around her desk and adjusted the mini-blinds at the window. As she fussed with other items in the room, she continued talking.

"I just don't believe that heart-attack stuff. Phil's body wouldn't have let him down like that."

Returning to her chair, Sigrid said, "But if the police wake up and start considering this a murder, I'm not going to have an alibi. I was supposed to go to a meeting that night, but I felt so bad after what had happened at the gala that I called and said I had the flu. After all, Phil's accusations were going to have serious repercussions for my career. I needed to sort things out. In fact, I hadn't even gone to work that day. I did call in, but those two calls were the only contacts I had all day."

"There hasn't been much in the papers about Stevenson's death," Charlotte said. "Do you know why he was at Columbus Central?"

"Knowing Phil, I'll bet it had something to do with the fake," Sigrid suggested. "I suppose we'll never know, though."

As Charlotte drove to the library later—a return trip made necessary by Ransom's lie—she thought over what she'd just found out from Sigrid. Melanie certainly hadn't mentioned Phil's affairs to her. Had he had one too many? She found it interesting that both of the women she knew to be romantically involved with Phil—Melanie and Sigrid— were adamant that he didn't have a heart attack. As Sigrid had put it, "Phil's body wouldn't have let him down like that." Old Phil must have been quite a lover, Charlotte thought.

If Sigrid had been in love with Phil, she certainly had a motive for killing him, once he dumped her. Or maybe the motive was to protect the project that was important to her career. Since she didn't have an alibi, she could have had the opportunity. And, at six feet and with her conditioning program, her height and strength could have made her a formidable opponent.

The earliest article about Ransom she found in the library

was published in June 1976 in the business section of the *Citizen-Journal,* a now defunct morning newspaper. The story announced his arrival at Alliance, and said he had previously been employed at the Toledo Museum of Art, having first majored in both art history and business administration in college. A sensible double major for someone who would end up specializing in insuring works of art, Charlotte thought.

A personality profile on Ransom, dating from the same time, appeared in the *Call and Post,* Columbus's weekly newspaper that covered the black community. Charlotte read that Ransom had been married and divorced before moving to Columbus. The article also mentioned that Ransom was becoming quite an art collector.

Subsequent articles on Ransom appeared in several publications, most of them having to do with his duties as a member of the board of the Ohio Arts Consortium, which was a loose federation of local arts organizations. In addition, there had been an announcement of his promotion when he assumed his current position at Alliance in 1982 and several articles about society functions in which he was mentioned and even photographed.

Charlotte went back to her office and phoned Adam Walker at the Riverside Medical Building. She wanted to talk with him about the book he had recommended to Ransom and to see what else she could find out. However, his receptionist told her he wasn't there. Wednesday was one of his days for surgery at the hospital. Or for racquetball at the club, Charlotte thought.

Thursday

It wasn't until the next evening that Charlotte had more time to spend on the necklace articles. She sat in her living room, the copies of newspaper and magazine articles she had printed at the library spread around the couch where she sat. Periodically, her work was interrupted by Walt's and Ty's cheers from the den, where they were watching an NCAA basketball tournament game.

In a notebook, Charlotte was creating a matrix of the information she had obtained about her suspects. Suspects' names were listed down the left side of the page. Across the top she had listed "Alibi," "Possible Motive," and "Miscellaneous." She was filling in each block with the information she had gathered. She marked some of them as needing further verification.

As far as her suspects' alibis were concerned, only Daphne Walker seemed totally in the clear by having been at the Chamber of Commerce meeting. Consequently, Charlotte resolved not to consider her a suspect any longer. She still needed to figure out a way to verify that Libby Fox and Barry Abrams had been in their offices when Phil was killed, that Sigrid Olson had been at home, and that Adam Walker had been writing up case notes at his office. She had no idea where Richard Ransom had been that night, not having realized when she talked to him that he would turn out to be one of her suspects.

Now she tried to fill in the "Possible Motive" cells across from each name. In their roles as exhibit officials and sponsors, Libby, Barry, Sigrid, Adam, and perhaps Ransom could have been desperate enough for the show to succeed to have killed Phil to shut him up about the fake, she wrote. In addition, Sigrid could have killed him because he had ended their affair.

She supposed that Libby, Barry, or Sigrid could have stolen the necklace for its monetary value. Adam and Ransom seemed too wealthy to risk stealing art for resale, but anything was possible.

Under "Miscellaneous," she wrote, "family China connection" and "art theft conversation with Ransom" in Adam Walker's cell; "brawler" and "previous Chinese art show" in Barry's; "bigger and stronger than most men" in Sigrid's; "knew there was something wrong with the necklace but didn't do anything about it" in Libby's; and "lie about insurance coverage" in Ransom's.

It felt good to have the information spelled out on paper, but there were still so many blanks to be filled in.

Friday

Not really sure what her next step should be, Charlotte decided to spend the next morning visiting the Campbell collection at the Wexner Center on Ohio State's campus. The collection contained the Chinese artifacts brought back by Adam's missionary grandparents. To prepare, she reread the newspaper articles about Adam. She turned the information over and over in her mind, and finally realized what was bothering her: her assumption that Margot Walker had died, simply because Daphne was Catholic. If Walker's first wife was alive, Charlotte wanted to talk with her. She needed some proof that Margot had indeed died. How to get it?

She considered phoning everybody with Margot's maiden name—Carr—living in Bellefontaine, Margot's hometown as mentioned in one of the articles. But the thought of asking strangers about the whereabouts of what was likely to be a dead relative did not seem like a particularly good idea.

So Charlotte drove downtown to the Ohio Division of Vital Statistics on Front Street, in what was one of her favorite buildings. As she pulled open the heavy doors and entered the marble lobby, she ignored the colorful mosaics on the ceiling and walls and didn't even consider going to look at the bronze portraits of Ohio's eight United States presidents that lined one west corridor.

Instead she walked quickly downstairs, passed the bronze portraits of Ohio Indian chiefs Pontiac, Tecumseh, Logan, and Little Turtle, and found room G-20, which was marked with an old-fashioned lighted sign that read "Birth Certificates."

She had to wait a few moments for the man ahead of her to finish his business, but then she was able to ask the middle-aged woman behind the counter how she could get a copy of a death certificate.

"Did your deceased die in Ohio?" the woman asked.

Charlotte said "yes," as if she knew, because she *did* know that the only death records kept by the division were on people declared dead within the state.

The woman asked whether the deceased had died before December 20, 1908. Charlotte really did know the answer to that one.

"Good," the woman said. "The records of those who died before that date are kept at the Ohio Historical Society. Just fill out one of these yellow forms and bring it to me when you're finished."

Charlotte sat down at one of the school desks in the narrow room and did her best with the form. However, two important pieces of information were unavailable to her: the year and Ohio county of Margot's death. She left blank the space for the county and wrote in "since 1963" in the space for "year of death," recalling that the photo of Margot at the donation ceremonies had been published in 1964.

The clerk told Charlotte there would be a seven-dollar charge for each certified copy she wanted of the record and then took the form through a door to her left, through which Charlotte could see other people working at computer terminals.

The search took about fifteen minutes and produced no death certificate for Margot Carr Walker. The clerk suggested that Charlotte return when she knew the county and year in which her deceased had died. Charlotte thanked her and thought again that perhaps she didn't *have* a deceased.

On the way to the Wexner Center, she thought carefully about all the reasons Margot's death certificate would not have shown up at the Ohio Division of Vital Statistics.

One, she died outside of Ohio. Two, perhaps she died in Ohio but the computer couldn't find the death record without the county or precise year of death. Three, she had not died.

Suddenly Charlotte thought of another way to track down the elusive Margot Carr Walker and abruptly steered the car toward I-70 and Whitehall, a suburb east of Columbus. Her destination was the Ohio Nurses Association headquarters. A living Margot would appear in the ONA directory only if she had remained a nurse, if she worked in Ohio, and if she was a member. Several big ifs, but it was all Charlotte had to go on.

Charlotte was confident that the ONA would be willing to help her because the association's executive director was an old friend, Ami Huston. She and Ami had served together on various committees and had long shared the desire to see nurses get the credit that they and other denizens of the "pink collar ghetto" deserved.

Ami did help, and to Charlotte's delight, a search through the ONA computerized directory revealed not only that Margot was very much alive, but that she was a nursing supervisor at Miami Valley Hospital in Dayton. She had apparently remarried, because her last name was now Paretsky. The search had been successful because the ONA, being an organization whose members were mostly women, was accustomed to hanging on to member's maiden as well as married names.

Ami was even willing to provide Margot's address and phone number. However, she told Charlotte that she would deny ever having used the resources of the ONA to cooperate with Charlotte if Charlotte revealed the source of her information about Margot. Charlotte said she understood entirely, thanked Ami, told her she hoped to return the favor someday, and sped back to Columbus and the Wexner Center.

In the gallery offices she found curator Gregory Louder, who said she should begin by reading a complete description of the items in the Campbell collection. Then she could request specific items she wanted to examine.

From the newspaper articles she had read earlier, Charlotte knew that Adam's maternal grandparents, Mary and George Otto Campbell, had been missionaries in Shantung Province from 1889 to 1900, sponsored by the Methodist Board of Foreign Missions in China. When they arrived overseas, Mary had been twenty years old and Otto twenty-three, and they had been married less than a year. Adam's uncle Carl had been born in China about five years later, but his mother, Sarah, had been born after the Campbells returned to the United States.

Now Charlotte sat reading the list of items the family had brought back with them after being expelled from China during the Boxer Rebellion eleven years after they began their missionary work. The list included family diaries.

Deciding to start with the diaries, Charlotte requested them from the Wexner staff. In a few moments she was reading a typed transcript of the journals written by Mary and George Campbell from their arrival in China until 1902, a short time after their return to the United States.

Charlotte was transfixed by the descriptions of the Campbells' life in China. In educated prose of the late-nineteenth century, the diaries detailed the Campbells' pleasure at their arrival; their religious commitment; their appreciation of Chinese culture; the minutiae of everyday life in the mission as they worked to convert Chinese souls to Christianity; the gratitude of Chinese people for the medical, agricultural, and spiritual help the family offered. Eventually, there was an account of the Campbells' flight from China to avoid what was likely to be death at the hands of the Boxers, China's anti-Christian, anti-foreigner faction.

It was a fascinating account, and more than once Charlotte had to subdue her desire to pace about the room as she read.

The last entries described the interest shown the returning missionaries by the Methodist Church hierarchy and congregations. And while the Campbells appreciated the interest and attention, it sounded as if they would rather have been in China.

Because she had to meet Conor Ennis for her jazz article, Charlotte never got any further than the Campbell diaries. While Ennis turned out to be a pleasant interviewee who gave her several interesting quotes, Charlotte had to struggle to concentrate, her mind still in China with the Campbells.

23

"C 'mon, Charlotte. Onion rings."

Walt stood in the doorway of the second-floor office, where Charlotte had sequestered herself since early that morning: her deadline for the jazz article was Monday.

Walt and Tyler had run all the errands that had piled up during the week, including replenishing the coffee supply that was keeping her going and providing a huge salad for her lunch. Now, Tyler was safely off at Kevin's house, working on beating the newest Nintendo game, and Walt was ready for a break.

"I haven't heard any keyboarding for over ten minutes. Either you've finished or you've run out of inspiration. Let's go to the Blue and get you some onion rings."

Walt stayed in the doorway, not about to chance a sprained ankle by wading across the piles of opened books and notes spread out on the floor.

Charlotte shook her head violently, as though to clear out the past hours' work, and said, "What?"

Walt patiently replied, "Let's go to the Blue and get you some onion rings."

"Oh. Okay. I seem to have run out of steam."

The Blue Danube was a restaurant on North High Street, not far from the Samses' Clintonville home. Charlotte had been eating at the Blue since she was an undergraduate journalism student at Ohio State almost twenty years earlier. The J-school students often gathered at the Blue after putting the *Ohio State Lantern,* the university's student-run daily newspaper, to bed.

Soon after they met as volunteers on a Senate campaign, Charlotte had taken Walt to the restaurant, and now, some fifteen years later, they still believed that the Blue made the best onion rings in the city.

She took the time to splash some cold water on her face, run a comb through her hair, and decide that her navy-blue velour sweats were perfectly acceptable attire for the Blue. When she and Walt were seated in their favorite booth with the cracked red plastic seats, they didn't need to look at the menu.

"I'll have a turkey sandwich, an order of onion rings, and a Heineken," Walt told the waitress. "Charlotte, what about you?"

"The same sandwich for me, but make it a double order of onion rings and a diet Coke."

As they ate, Walt filled Charlotte in on what he and Tyler had accomplished during the day. In addition to the grocery shopping, they had picked up the camping equipment Tyler would need for the Boy Scout trek scheduled for next month, a box of paper for the computer, and some other odds and ends.

After Tyler had been deposited at Kevin's, Walt had dived into the book of cryptoquotes he'd picked up at the bookstore. Charlotte didn't especially want to hear him complain about the low difficulty level of the puzzles, since, despite her occupation, she was not very good at word games.

"I sure wish all my puzzles had easy answers," Charlotte said a bit petulantly. "This article is driving me crazy. Maybe I'm just distracted by the murder."

She watched as Walt's face assumed what she called his "long-suffering" look. He had never agreed with her conviction that Phil had been murdered, even after the threatening call and the broken figurine. "There are just too many other explanations for what you insist on calling your 'death threats,' " he had said.

As Charlotte was savoring the onion rings, a woman walked past their booth toward the rest rooms.

"Walt!" Charlotte grabbed his hand across the table. "That's Melanie! What on earth is she doing up here on this side of town at this hour on a Saturday night? And less than a week after Phil's funeral. Where are the kids? She surely hasn't brought them with her. Who is she with?"

"Simmer down, Charlotte. Are you sure it was Melanie? The light in here isn't all that good."

"I'm sure it's her," Charlotte hissed, keeping her voice level down with difficulty. "I'm going to stand up to see who's in those front booths, and then I'm going to the rest room, too."

Charlotte stood, gazed over the tops of the booths, and sat down with a thud. "It's Barry Abrams, Walt," she whispered, stunned. "He's the manager of the Son of Heaven exhibit, remember? The one who objected to having the necklace tested. The one who was supposed to be working in his office at Central the night Phil died there." The one who had familiarly ruffled Lionel's hair at Phil's memorial service, she said to herself.

Before Walt had a chance to do anything more than open his mouth, Charlotte was out of the booth and headed for the rest room. She entered as Melanie was washing her hands.

"Charlotte!" Melanie gasped. "What are you doing here?"

"I might ask you the same question," responded Charlotte. "In fact, I will: What *are* you doing here with Barry Abrams?"

"Oh, dear. You saw Barry? He was so sure that nobody would recognize him if we came here. None of the arts crowd would be caught dead here, he said. We usually just go to his place, but we wanted to do something different tonight—"

"Usually? How long have you been involved with this

guy?" Without waiting for Melanie to reply, Charlotte said, "I can't believe it. Good little Melanie with her clean little house and her good little children—"

"And her big bad husband who had affairs for years. You didn't really think I believed that stuff about him having to work all night, did you? The Sigrid Olson thing was the last straw. That's why I started with Barry. To get even."

"Did Phil know about this?"

"I'm sure he didn't. We only got together when Phil was tied up with classes or having to 'work' all night. We never went out in public."

"I don't understand how you were getting even if Phil didn't know about it."

"I knew about it. That's what was important. That somebody found me attractive enough to be with me as a person. Not just a housekeeper and mother."

"How did you meet Barry? I thought Phil pretty much kept you out of the art world," said Charlotte.

"He did. We met at the grocery store. Barry's apartment is not far from the store I usually go to. One of my neighbors introduced me to him about six months ago. We just stood there in the aisle and talked and talked. He asked me up for coffee and we've been getting together ever since."

"Does Barry think this is serious? Serious enough to have wanted Phil out of the way so that you could marry him?" Charlotte asked, remembering Barry's lack of a corroborated alibi for the evening Phil had died.

"Barry would never have murdered Phil," Melanie insisted. "Never, never, never. He's such a sweet, gentle person."

Suspecting that was not the case, Charlotte simply stared at Melanie, who suddenly grabbed Charlotte's arm. "I'm sure Barry had nothing to do with Phil's death," she said vehemently. "Please don't tell anybody what I've told you tonight. Please."

Charlotte nodded. Melanie quickly left the rest room, and Charlotte followed a moment later.

Back in her booth, Charlotte took the notebook out of her purse and wrote "affair with Melanie" in the block across from Barry's name in the column "Possible Motive."

And then, as Walt systematically ate her extra order of onion rings, she considered the grid as a whole and realized that she had made a very basic mistake: she had assumed that when two things occur together, one is the cause of the other. She had assumed that because Phil had identified the fake necklace and then died, his murderer had been the person who had stolen the real necklace. Now she realized that the necklace theft and the murder could be two entirely separate crimes.

24

Monday

Charlotte walked out onto the porch, popped an audio-cassette into her Walkman, and pulled on the earphones. Pushing the "on" button, she smiled unconsciously as the deep, carefully dictioned voice of an English actor filled her ears with the script of the Dick Francis mystery he was reading. This was probably the fifth unabridged Francis mystery she had heard this actor read as she walked forty-five minutes every morning before leaving for work. By now the sound of his voice was as welcome as an old friend's.

The area in which she walked was just south of Whetstone Park, between High Street and the Olentangy River. She turned off Amazon Road and onto Milton. For some reason, all the east-west streets there had sidewalks, but Milton and Olentangy Boulevard, the only north-south streets on that side of High, did not.

An occasional car went by. Charlotte was vaguely aware of a blue one passing slowly. Most of her attention was on the Dick Francis mystery as she walked at the edge of the road and watched a tabby cat stalk a bird in the yard to her right.

Suddenly she saw a flash of blue out of the corner of her eye, and she jumped off to the right to avoid the car that careened on down the road. That had been close. It had been more than close. Her left arm ached and she flexed it experimentally. Nothing broken, apparently. The sleeve of her jacket was torn where it buttoned at the cuff. She guessed the car's mirror had caught it. Thank heavens it had torn. Otherwise she would have been slammed into the side of the car. She was so shaken that she sat down on the grass, feeling sick to her stomach.

Maybe Walt was right, she thought ruefully. Exercise *could* kill you.

There was no sign of the blue car. What fool would drive so carelessly through a residential neighborhood? she thought angrily. Then a disturbing question came to mind: What makes you so sure it was carelessness? Maybe the only careless part was that he missed. Maybe this was the next step following the threatening call and the broken figurine. Maybe the blue car was going to come *back* for another go at her as soon as it turned around.

There was an awful pounding in Charlotte's chest as she got to her feet and tried desperately to think of the shortest route home. Impulsively, she turned up Erie Road and half-ran toward High Street. Every car that passed struck her as suspicious, and she compulsively looked over her shoulder every few minutes. Her breath was coming in great gasps. She concentrated on getting it under control.

Taking action helped restore her equilibrium. She considered leaving the plainly visible sidewalk to seek the protection of the shrubs next to the houses along her route. But the vision of herself creeping from shrub to shrub struck her as funny, and the humor made her feel a little better.

As she walked, Charlotte cursed Phil Stevenson. Why hadn't he kept his mouth shut about the fake? For that matter, why hadn't she kept *her* mouth shut about the necklace?

Fifteen minutes later her front porch was visible, and Charlotte ran the last forty yards as fast as she could. She hurled herself onto the porch and through the front door.

Heading for the kitchen at the back of the house, she

yelled several times for Walt. She found him before he could reach her, having half-risen from the kitchen table at the sound of her frantic voice. He looked alarmed, and Charlotte was instantly grateful for his concern.

Quickly she told him about the blue car grazing her arm and about her desperate flight home. As it became clear to him that Charlotte was unhurt, Walt's concern seemed to turn to exasperation. The first thing he said, once Charlotte had finished, was "It's those damn earphones!"

Taken aback, she asked, "Who said anything about earphones?"

"I did. I tell you all the time that they're dangerous because they keep you from hearing what's going on around you. And then you walk in traffic only half paying attention. You could have been killed, Charlotte!"

"How come you aren't calling the driver who almost hit me dangerous?"

"All right: he's dangerous, too. But he's got nothing to do with Phil. There's not one chance in a thousand that he's involved in Phil's death. He's probably just some careless slob who drives to work half asleep every morning. And that's why you have to stop wearing those stupid earphones—so you can protect yourself from dangerous drivers like him."

"I can't believe you think this is somehow my fault," Charlotte said angrily, beginning to pace around the kitchen. "Talk about blaming the victim!" She threw a pot into the sink, making a satisfying clatter.

"I'm not blaming anybody. No, I'm blaming the driver, of course. But . . . you've heard people tell drivers to drive defensively? I'm telling you that you have to walk defensively, Charlotte."

"Honestly, this is so patronizing."

Walt realized that his worry over Charlotte's safety was causing him to lecture. Why, after all these years, he thought, did he forget how much she resented the slightest hint of condescension? Every now and then he seemed to blunder into these stupid exchanges that, on later reflection, he had to admit she should find offensive. As she paced past him, he caught one of her hands and pulled her to him and apologized.

Unmollified, she pulled away. "I'm surprised that you don't think I made the whole thing up."

"Of course not."

"Then why don't you believe that this driver deliberately tried to hit me?"

"You could be right, Charlotte. But it just seems like an overreaction to me. You were walking on a street that has no sidewalks, right?"

"Yes."

"Then it's not like the driver had to make his car jump the curb to come so close, is it?"

Reluctantly, she nodded.

"And you said you didn't see the blue car on the way home. Even though you took a different street, he could have found you easily—if he was really trying to get you."

"You wouldn't be saying that if you had been there. Or if he had come after you."

"Maybe you're right. But if you hadn't had those earphones on, you would have heard him coming. Why don't you leave them at home for a while?"

Leave the earphones at home? Charlotte thought incredulously. Didn't this man realize she was going to stay home herself as much as possible, lest the driver of the blue car succeed the next time? To Walt, she merely said she'd think about skipping the earphones.

Later, she tried to remember whether any of her suspects drove blue cars. Sigrid did, she knew, but she thought that Sigrid's car seemed newer than the car that had tried to hit her. And she seemed to recall that the driver of that car was a man, not a woman. Of course, a suspect could have hired somebody else to run her down. And then the color of the car would be irrelevant. Resolutely, a frightened Charlotte decided to stop her necklace investigation.

25

Wednesday

Lou Toreson arrived at the Son of Heaven exhibit for the second day in a row to guide groups of students through the show. Business had been so brisk that volunteers had been asked to contribute extra days.

To her surprise, Daphne Walker was seated on one of the folding chairs just outside the "auspicious" doors to the exhibit. Lou noted that the perfectly groomed Daphne managed to look as elegant in the mandarin jacket as she had at the gala.

Lou said hello, sat down next to her, and asked if she was a regular Wednesday tour guide. Daphne seemed quite ill at ease.

"No," she stated emphatically, "I'm not. I mean, I only take groups of adults through the museum. I'm not a Son of Heaven regular. They're so short-handed here that I agreed to help out, but I'm not looking forward to these children."

Lou remembered that Daphne had mentioned her disinterest in children during her survey interview.

"I don't even know whether I can handle these brats," Daphne said.

Noting how Daphne's discomfort seemed to be escalating, Lou began to worry that she was not in any condition to escort thirty lively middle-school kids through the exhibit.

She tried to think of some way to calm her down. Noting that the first contingent of students was still viewing the slide show and that, as additions, she and Daphne were well down on the volunteer list, Lou suggested that they tell the team captain they were going to the lounge for tea. Daphne readily agreed.

Once they were seated with their drinks, Lou cast about for a topic to help Daphne relax. She decided they had nothing in common except, perhaps, their interest in the Son of Heaven show. So she finally asked whether any of the Columbus Son of Heaven sponsors had seen the exhibit when it was in Seattle, perhaps as a preview before committing themselves here. It was a shot in the dark that paid off unexpectedly.

Daphne seemed to calm down a bit as she told Lou in some detail about the trip she and Adam had made to Seattle the previous June. But she began to seem agitated again by the time she got to the part about Adam's having made another trip out there in November. "I didn't go with him," she said. "By then, he'd fallen head over heels in love with that scrawny child who works as his receptionist. She probably went."

"Oh," Lou said, taken aback by Daphne's candor. "I saw you with Dr. Walker at the Son of Heaven dinner. I had no idea, of course—"

"I'm letting him stay at the apartment and we're still appearing in public together for some of our social obligations," Daphne interjected. "But that's just until the divorce settlement is completely worked out. Of course, thanks to Daddy, we had a pre-nuptial agreement about *my* money, but I think I should get the Waterford place and part of his professional earnings."

"You probably enhanced his earning power by entertaining and so on," Lou said, trying to sound sincere.

"I made sure he met all the right people," Daphne agreed. "We had a partnership. After that disastrous first marriage of his, Adam didn't really want a love match. Neither did

I, for that matter; just a handsome man to escort me, provide sex, and look good to the people that matter."

Lou was more than a little startled at this cold-blooded approach to marriage.

"I don't know what happened to him," Daphne went on. "He claims he's fallen in love with her. Maybe he wants to have children to keep his name alive. Oprah says that men Adam's age—he's fifty-five—start worrying about mortality."

Lou sipped her tea, wondering how long it had been since Daphne had had such an attentive audience.

"I certainly made it clear to him before we were married that I had no intention of having any children, and he agreed with me entirely."

Abruptly, Daphne said, "You know, Lou, I really can't face taking those noisy kids through the exhibition. Would you tell the team captain I've had to leave?"

Lou said she would and then they headed back, Daphne to return the jacket to the volunteer headquarters room and Lou to rejoin the group of additional volunteers.

It was a good thing that the tour script was so firmly ingrained in Lou's memory. Otherwise Daphne's revelations, including her unemotional view of marriage, would have made it difficult for her to have talked about the Chinese exhibits for the next two hours. Never one to romanticize the institution of marriage, Lou nonetheless wondered what had led Daphne and Adam into such a long-standing, though lukewarm, arrangement. Perhaps this detached relationship had resulted in the kind of over-organization that Daphne had displayed during their earlier interview.

After finishing her tour-guide duties, Lou stopped by Charlotte's office on the way home. Because she had been out of town for a couple of days, Lou had not heard about Charlotte's incident with the blue car until Charlotte called last night. Charlotte had still been frightened and, not incidentally, furious with Walt for not believing her that the almost-accident had been deliberate. Lou was anxious to make sure Charlotte was feeling better by this time and to pass on the information from Daphne.

She found her friend pounding away more ferociously than usual at her computer. When Lou commented on her intensity, Charlotte told her she was trying to make up for lost time.

"I've been so preoccupied with Phil's death and the necklace articles that I've let everything else slip," she said.

"Well, speaking of your necklace investigation, I learned this morning that Daphne and Adam Walker are getting a divorce."

Charlotte didn't act as interested as Lou would have predicted, but she did ask, "How good is your source?"

"Daphne herself. According to her, Adam has fallen in love with his receptionist. Daphne called her 'that scrawny child' and said she and Adam had probably visited the Son of Heaven show while it was in Seattle."

"Poor Daphne," Charlotte said.

"Don't waste your sympathy on Daphne, Char. She made it plain to me that she's upset only because she's losing an attractive escort for all the right parties and a sex partner, not because she loves him."

"That's even sadder. She and Adam must be quite a pair."

"To hear Daphne tell it, their marriage has been strictly business."

"But if Adam is so calculating and cold, how can Daphne believe that he's in love with his receptionist?"

"Don't ask me to explain these people, Charlotte. The Walkers are still living together until they get the divorce settlement worked out. Daphne says she's demanding a percentage of his professional earnings during the time they were married because her social contacts helped his practice."

"He's probably made a mint."

"Maybe he'll have to part with some of his art collection. Of course, that could be Daphne's."

"Personally, I'm a little sick of art at the moment," Charlotte said. "And I'm sorry I ever had reason to meet the Walkers."

"What's wrong?"

"I just don't think I can take any more phone threats, weird packages, and blue cars trying to run me down."

To Charlotte's relief, Lou was sympathetic and seemed to need no convincing that all those things were related to the fake necklace and Phil's death.

"As far as I'm concerned, Columbus will just have to get along without knowing there was a fake in the Son of Heaven show," Charlotte concluded.

"This isn't like you, Char. You usually hang on to your projects until the bitter end."

"I know. But this time I'm truly frightened."

"But what will you gain by stopping now? How will the killer even know that you've stopped? Do you intend to take out an ad in the paper saying, 'I quit. Stop trying to kill me'?"

"No, of course not, but—"

"And for the rest of your life you're going to have to look over your shoulder, worrying. Because whoever is threatening you knows that you can't 'un-know' what you've learned about the necklace."

Charlotte had started pacing around the room, which was a good sign. This was the Charlotte Lou was used to.

"And as far as Walt is concerned, and even that detective who ignored you—what do they matter? You may be angry at them for not having faith in you, but what would you have actually done differently if they had believed you from the beginning?"

Charlotte clearly recalled that Lou also had not believed her earlier, but didn't mention it. "Nothing, probably," she answered.

"Right. They're irrelevant. Or should be."

"But I'm afraid."

"I don't blame you. But you've got the makings of a great

article here, and you're a fool if you let it slip through your fingers."

Lou's words did the trick. After she left, Charlotte dug her notebook out of the wastepaper can and looked over the matrix. By the time she had penciled in the new information about the Walker divorce, she was hooked again. She paced about, considering whether the divorce information changed anything, eventually deciding that it provided a possible motive for Adam as the necklace thief: need for money.

Assuming Daphne won her settlement, she'd share in anything she could prove he'd made while they were married. So what he needed was not just cash but *unaccountable* cash—money Daphne couldn't get her hands on. And the sale of a stolen necklace to an unreputable dealer could provide that money.

Charlotte left her office determined to talk to Adam's receptionist. She was glad it was Wednesday, since this was Adam's day for surgery and she should have the receptionist to herself.

She walked into Walker's first-floor office and approached the blue-eyed receptionist seated behind a low counter that formed the wall between her desk and the waiting room. The young woman's thick blond hair fell in curly cascades past her shoulders. Her makeup was skillfully applied but overdone: too much eye shadow, too much blush, too red a lipstick. Because her desk was almost entirely free of work-related paraphernalia, Charlotte assumed she was there chiefly to look good, sort of a living testimonial to the surgeon's greatness. And maybe even answer the phone on occasion, too. Judging from the bottles on her desk, doing her nails was also part of her job. Charlotte told her she had just come from her dentist's office in the building and had taken a chance that she could make an appointment to discuss "having some cosmetic surgery done."

She purposefully did not say what *kind* of cosmetic surgery, and the receptionist did not ask. However, her eyes swept over Charlotte's body and Charlotte imagined she saw the word "liposuction" forming like a light bulb over her blond head.

All she said to Charlotte was, "Won't you come in and sit down for a moment," indicating a chair next to her own desk. "In" was a small office that held the receptionist's desk, a few chairs, and several lateral filing cabinets.

As Charlotte sat down, the receptionist said, "There isn't anybody else back here today, and it seemed silly to have you stand out there."

"Not even the doctor is here today?" Charlotte asked, just to be sure.

The receptionist said no and explained, as she had a week ago on the phone, about Wednesday being Walker's day for surgery at Riverside Hospital. Charlotte was relieved and decided that she could afford to play her role a little broader.

In vain, she studied the woman's chic white dress (surely it couldn't be called a uniform) for a name badge. She finally found a nameplate on the desk. Tiffany Shore.

Tiffany flipped open an appointment book. Charlotte settled back in her chair and, banking on the apparent need of the young to be constantly entertained, said, "I suppose it's pretty boring for you on Wednesdays, Tiffany." She looked expectantly at her, adding, "What with this empty office and nobody to talk to."

Tiffany shifted her concentration from the appointment book to Charlotte. "Boy, you're right about that. Sometimes I think I'll just flip out."

"Why don't you just close the office on Wednesdays?"

"Ad—— Dr. Walker wouldn't hear of that. Of course it's me, not him, who's stuck here with nothing to do but answer the phone and do a little filing."

Tiffany had found the first appointment opening. It was in mid-May, nearly two months away. She asked Charlotte if that day and time were all right with her, and Charlotte agreed automatically. When Tiffany asked for her name, Charlotte casually replied "Carolyn Kroll" and spelled the last name for her. Then she concocted a phone number.

"I hope I'm recovered from this surgery by the fall," she told Tiffany chattily. "I'm going to visit my sister in Seattle in October, and I'd like any bruising or pain to be over with. Do you think I'll be all finished by then?"

"I really couldn't say. You'll have to ask the doctor those kinds of questions."

"I'm really looking forward to this trip. I haven't been to the West Coast before, and—

"I was in Seattle last November," Tiffany volunteered.

Bless you, child, Charlotte thought. "Oh, really? How did you like it?"

"Okay, I guess. We were out there for a medical convention, my boyfriend and me. He had to be in all those meetings during the day. I mostly watched TV in the hotel room. Don't figure I missed much. We got to eat in some nice restaurants while we were there, though."

"If you remember the names of any of those restaurants, I'll jot them down," Charlotte prompted.

"Oh, I don't remember them now. Except one was in that Space Needle thing they have out there. It was near our hotel. Anyway," Tiffany said, tossing her hair out of her eyes, "I liked L.A. better. We flew down there after Seattle, the day before Thanksgiving."

"Sounds like a nice trip," Charlotte said, remembering that the Son of Heaven exhibit was housed in Seattle's Flag Center on the former site of the World's Fair, which included the Space Needle, of course. Near their hotel, Tiffany had said.

Charlotte wondered whether the hotel was one connected with the medical convention or whether Adam Walker had chosen it in order to be near the exhibit. She was afraid to ask.

The conversation seemed to have died a natural death.

Trying to come up with something to prolong it, Charlotte finally said, "Two months is an awfully long time to have to wait for an appointment. I could lose my nerve by then."

Tiffany smiled reassuringly, perhaps even patronizingly, at the older, plumper Charlotte. "There's nothing to worry about. Cosmetic surgery is very safe and Dr. Walker is very good at it. He did my breasts."

I bet he did, thought Charlotte, but resisted the impulse to say anything other than "That's nice." What *does* one say? she thought.

"Do you take 'before' and 'after' pictures of your patients?" she then asked. Tiffany said they did.

"Maybe you could show me some and help me get an idea of the difference cosmetic surgery can make."

"You mean now?"

Charlotte nodded.

"But the doctor always shows those to patients during their first appointment," Tiffany said. "I don't think he'd want me to be jumping ahead in our routine."

"Well," Charlotte said, thinking fast, "the kind of surgery I want won't involve my face. So maybe you could just show me some pictures of people who had *facial* surgery. That way, I'll be able to see the effects of some successful surgery, and you won't be showing me the pictures the doctor will want to go over with me later."

She looked at Tiffany to see if she had followed all that. Tiffany bought it. Smiling, she said she'd get the pictures, rose from her desk, and went through a doorway that Charlotte assumed led to examining rooms.

Tiffany soon came back with a photo album, which she handed to Charlotte. Inside were color photos of the faces of perhaps thirty women before and after their surgery, presumably at the hands of Dr. Walker. Judging from the "before" photos, these women were scheduled for face and neck lifts, eyelid tucks and bag removal, nose jobs, or chin reshaping. All of them looked dramatically better in the "after" shots. But then they should, Charlotte noted, considering that in the "before" photos they appeared with no makeup and with their hair brushed back, away from their faces. The shots showed nothing below their shoulders, but it looked as if they had not been wearing blouses. Consequently, their faces looked naked, too.

In contrast, the "after" photos showed them with full makeup and with earrings. Collars of their mostly off-camera blouses nicely framed their faces, and necklaces were visible on some. It looked as if several women had had their hair styled for the photo session.

Charlotte oohed and aahed appreciatively over the skill of the surgeon who had wrought such changes in these patients, and Tiffany beamed.

Tiffany seemed to enjoy having someone to talk with, and they continued chatting companionably over the pictures for the next twenty minutes or so. During that time, Charlotte steered the conversation back to Seattle. She reminded Tiffany that the Son of Heaven exhibit had been there at the same time she and her boyfriend were. Had they seen it? she asked.

Tiffany said that her boyfriend had seen it twice while they were there. Both times were in the evening, and he had insisted that Tiffany not accompany him. He had told her that she couldn't possibly enjoy the exhibit, since it would only bore someone her age. ("My boyfriend's a lot older than me," she explained in a confidential voice.)

She told Charlotte that at first she had not believed him and had worried that he was seeing another woman—perhaps someone he had met at the convention. But she finally had to admit that maybe he knew what he was talking about, once she viewed the show in Columbus. It *was* boring.

Before Charlotte could defend the show, the phone rang and, from Tiffany's tone of voice, she judged it was the doctor. Time to go. Charlotte picked up her purse, mouthed the word "good-bye" in Tiffany's direction, and left.

26

Walking up the front steps to her house later, Charlotte could tell that nobody else was there. The place had that locked-up look, even though Walt should have been home from work by then and Tyler had not mentioned any activity when she had talked with him after school.

She walked across the wide front porch, turned the key in the lock, and pushed the door open. She was right about the house being empty, but on the hall table Walt had left a note explaining their absence. They had gone to the Boy Scout father-and-son dinner, which Charlotte knew had been scheduled for several weeks but had completely forgotten.

So she was on her own for the evening. She used to treasure these infrequent moments of solitude at home. But this was the first evening she had been home alone since the blue car had nearly run her down, and she was a little nervous.

She pulled a container of homemade vegetable soup out of the freezer, grateful for that recent weekend of frenzied cooking. She pried the frozen soup into a pan, added some water, and heated it on the stove. Two slices of Italian bread and a diet soda completed her preparations. Then she got out her notebook.

As she ate at the kitchen table, she mentally reviewed the

information in her matrix. If she thought only about the necklace theft—as opposed to a possible murder—most of her suspects could have had a motive if the monetary reward had been great enough. But Sigrid didn't seem likely to have had access to the necklace. Besides, why would she have done anything to hurt her first big project for CP&L?

That left Libby, Barry, and Adam—all of whom could have been tempted *and* had access to the necklace. But of the three, Adam seemed her best guess as necklace thief—especially since he had made those solo visits to the show in Seattle while Tiffany cooled her heels in their hotel room. And she shouldn't overlook his art-theft conversation with Ransom.

Of course, she reminded herself, *she* had had an art-theft conversation with Ransom, too.

Phil's murder—if there was a murder—was a different matter. Charlotte had trouble imagining the elegant plastic surgeon doing something as tacky as killing Phil Stevenson. Stealing a beautiful necklace, perhaps. Violating the Hippocratic oath to cover it up seemed much less likely.

She had far less trouble imagining the burly Barry Abrams, with his history of brawling, killing the obnoxious husband of the woman with whom he was having an affair. Particularly if he considered that husband to have mistreated his wife.

Ah, love, Charlotte thought. For it, Adam was divorcing his beautiful and wealthy wife. For it, Barry may have risked everything to kill Phil Stevenson. For it, Charlotte saved some vegetable soup for Walt, who at that moment was probably eating cold dry chicken and lumpy pudding at the Boy Scout banquet.

The front doorbell rang just when she had finished eating. She left the kitchen, walked through the darkened front hall, and cautiously looked out the small windows at the side of the front door. Without the porch light on, she could not identify the slight figure standing there with its back to the door. She turned on the porch light and looked again, relieved to see Melanie Stevenson staring back expectantly.

Melanie took off her jacket and tossed it on the hall tree. She preceded Charlotte into the living room, seated herself on the couch, and explained that she had come to check on the progress of Charlotte's investigation into Phil's death.

"Barry suggested I come over while he takes the kids to a movie," Melanie said.

"Barry knows I'm asking some questions about Phil's death?"

"Of course. I told him the moment you agreed to help me."

"Great, Mel. That's just great." Charlotte remembered that the threats had started immediately after she agreed to help Melanie.

"Why would you care whether Barry knows or not? I don't keep anything from him."

"I'm just not sure about him. How much do you really know about this guy?"

"Everything," Melanie said, "and don't call him 'this guy.' You act like he's some kind of suspect and I resent it."

"I just think you might be wise to get to know him a little better before blabbing about my questions regarding Phil's death," Charlotte said. "Just to be on the safe side."

"Well, I know everything about him and he already knows you're investigating. I tell him everything, and he doesn't keep anything from me either. Do you actually think I'd have an affair with someone who killed my husband?"

Charlotte tried to think of a soothing answer but, in the end, settled for the truth. "No, but I think it might have happened the other way around: someone you had an affair with might have killed your husband."

"What is it with you, Charlotte? How come you never like the men I'm involved with? You sure didn't like Phil, and now you don't like Barry. You think Walt's so much better?"

Yes, oh, yes, Charlotte said thankfully to herself. But to Melanie, she said, "I'm just worried about you, Mel."

"Well, don't be. Barry's a nice guy. And he treats me and the kids fine."

"How are the kids?" Charlotte asked.

"Fine. They're doing great, considering all they've been through lately." Then Melanie asked what she had found out so far.

Charlotte suddenly decided to follow her own advice about not blabbing what she knew. "Not much," she said.

"Come on, Charlotte. You must have found out *something.*"

"All right then," she began. "Phil was right. There was a fake in the Son of Heaven show, and I was able to prove that to the museum officials."

Melanie seemed unimpressed. "I'm not surprised. Phil said there was one."

Then Charlotte realized that Melanie would have already known about the necklace test because Barry would have told her. There was no need to feel bad about breaking her promise to Libby.

"What else have you learned?"

Charlotte considered for a moment and then said, "Just that several people—including your 'boyfriend'—had access to the necklace and a motive for killing Phil. Barry doesn't even have anyone who can corroborate his alibi the night Phil died. But the police still say Phil died of a heart attack."

"Maybe they're right."

Charlotte was incredulous. "You've changed your mind? After you twisted my arm to help you? After I've stopped doing any proper work to make a living so that I could concentrate on helping you out? *Now* you say you could have been mistaken about Phil being too healthy to have a heart attack?"

"What do I know about heart attacks?" Melanie said demurely. "Maybe I just didn't want to accept Phil's death when I insisted he was murdered. Anyway, I think you've asked enough questions. Let the police handle this."

"Oh no, you don't," Charlotte said fiercely. "You can't get me into this and then simply say "stop." Not after everything that has happened."

Melanie, too, was upset by now. "I mean it, Charlotte!" she said forcefully. "You're going too far and if you're not careful, you're going to mess everything up."

"Mess what up?" Charlotte asked.

"I just want to get on with my life. Just stop helping me!"

An angry Melanie jumped to her feet, ran into the hall, grabbed her jacket, and stormed out the front door.

Charlotte watched through the open door as she got into her car and sped down the street. Closing the door, she realized that Melanie must think she had discovered more than she really had about Phil's death.

Melanie seemed almost frantic to protect Barry from Charlotte's investigation. On second thought, maybe Melanie was protecting herself. Maybe her refusal to believe the autopsy report and her request for Charlotte's help were devices to draw suspicion away from herself.

Charlotte was sorry that she had not had time to ask Melanie about where she was the night Phil died. Perhaps his appointment at Central had been with his latest girlfriend. Melanie could have joined them there and killed Phil in a fit of jealous rage. Her newly revealed assertiveness made that seem possible. But could Melanie know how to precipitate a heart attack?

Her family came home soon. While Walt ate some soup and Charlotte allowed herself a second helping, Ty settled for ice cream. Before long, Ty was in bed and she was able to tell Walt about Melanie's brief but explosive visit.

"I don't understand how she gets mixed up with these characters," Walt said. "First Phil, and now this guy Abrams, who also seems belligerent."

"I know. There does seem to be a pattern. But then I don't understand anybody who's mixed up in this mess."

They put their bowls in the sink, turned off the downstairs lights, and climbed the stairs.

As they got ready for bed, Charlotte filled Walt in on the latest developments in the necklace-theft part of her investigation.

"I like the idea that Adam could have stolen the necklace to get some money he wouldn't have to share with Daphne. But what doesn't make sense is that the two of them are still sharing the condo and appearing socially together—all the while they're planning a divorce."

"Does this mean that if I fall hopelessly in love with my secretary and tell you I'm divorcing you, you won't go with me to the next Boy Scout parents' banquet?"

Charlotte smiled. "I guess the Walkers do operate on a different social level than we do."

"Who was it that said the rich are different? Fitzgerald, I think," Walt said.

"But the answer is still no. I wouldn't walk across the street with you if we were getting a divorce."

Walt yawned and got into bed.

Charlotte continued talking. "I'm telling you, there's something creepy and cold-blooded about all their arrangements and machinations."

"Well, Adam isn't cold-blooded about his receptionist. Quite the opposite."

"Right. But I wish you could see her. Daphne's right. Tiffany Shore *is* a scrawny child."

"I wouldn't expect Daphne to give her rave reviews."

"Well, you can expect worse than that from *me* if you take up with your secretary."

"Believe me, no one will ever accuse you of being cold-blooded, Charlotte," Walt said, smiling knowingly as he pulled back the covers for her.

27

The next three days passed uneventfully, and Charlotte had a perfect day for her drive to Margot Paretsky's home near Dayton. There was little traffic for the ninety-mile trip, and the temperature was unseasonably warm.

When she had phoned Margot earlier in the week, Charlotte had explained that she was a Columbus free-lance writer who was interested in the Campbell family history and considering writing a book on the subject. She wanted to talk with Margot about the women in the Campbell family, particularly Mary and Sarah. Margot was only one of several people she would eventually be interviewing, Charlotte had said.

Predictably, Margot had not jumped at the chance to talk about her ex-in-laws. Charlotte had had to stress the potential book's importance to Americans' understanding of such an exotic country as China.

Finally, Margot had agreed to see her, but, she cautioned, Charlotte must remember that she had been out of the Campbell-Walker family for over twenty years now. Charlotte had assured her that any family lore she could share would be helpful.

Now, as she rolled along Interstate 70 through the flat, prosperously farmed countryside, Charlotte was reminded that the United States stretched out like a tabletop all the way from east of Columbus to the Rocky Mountains. She turned south on Ohio Route 4 for the last third of the trip, moved quickly through Dayton's downtown, and turned into Oakwood, one of Dayton's southern suburbs and probably the wealthiest community in the area. Charlotte had grown up in a small town near Dayton, so she was familiar with the area. She knew that Orville and Wilbur Wright had made their home in Oakwood, not far from where she believed Margot's house to be.

The streets in Oakwood were tree-lined and bordered with large houses, if not mansions the size of the one the Wright brothers had occupied. Margot's street was no exception. Her house was a tri-level, set back from the road a good eighty feet and surrounded by winter-bare mature trees. The stucco-and-brick exterior was painted gray, with darker-gray shutters. The driveway curved for the last several yards toward an attached garage, and the garage door was up. Charlotte could see a late-model Pontiac parked inside. It had a Miami Valley Hospital parking sticker on the rear bumper, so she assumed the car belonged to Margot.

Margot answered the doorbell herself, greeting Charlotte warmly. Charlotte studied Margot as she followed her into the spacious living room. She had dark hair and eyes and looked to be about Adam Walker's age, although, unlike Adam, Margot had lines around her eyes and mouth. She was slender, and her jeans and maroon cotton turtleneck made her look considerably younger than the wrinkles would indicate.

Margot asked her to sit down, indicating the sofa. She said she would bring in some tea and then they could get started with the questions.

While Margot was out of the room, Charlotte had a short while to study her surroundings. White was the dominant color: white walls, white sheers at the windows, white plush carpet. Even the sofa was covered in a loose-woven white fabric that had dark-blue piping at the edges. The square glass coffee table contained a spherical vase filled with bright floppy blooms on long stems, and scattered across the table were many expensive-looking crystal paperweights.

Charlotte thought all that white was reminiscent of a hospital or laboratory, but she rather liked the effect. The large plants at the windows, the piping on the sofa, the bright flecks of color in some of the paperweights, and the colors on some large canvases on the walls nicely interrupted the monochromatic scheme.

After Margot returned and set out the tea, Charlotte began the interview. It quickly became obvious that whatever Margot thought about her ex-husband, she had great respect and affection for his mother, Sarah. His grandmother, Mary Campbell, had died before Margot had joined the family, but Margot had apparently spent considerable time learning about her from Sarah. Adam, Margot said, had not seemed very interested in the elder Campbells. In fact, she had gotten the distinct feeling that he thought they could have spent their time in better ways than saving souls in China.

At Charlotte's careful prodding, Margot was able to recall several stories about the family that illustrated Sarah's and Mary's independence and generosity. They sounded like likeable people.

After a half hour, Charlotte felt comfortable enough with Margot to broach the subject of Adam Walker himself. "I suppose the family was disappointed when you and Dr. Walker divorced," she began.

"Yes, I think they were," Margot said easily. "None of us saw it coming, certainly not me. I was pregnant with our son Charlie when Adam asked for the divorce. Of course, Charlie was several months old by the time the divorce actually came through."

Encouraged that Margot had not shut down when the subject of the divorce came up, Charlotte decided to press on. "It was a surprise to you when Dr. Walker wanted a divorce?"

"A complete surprise. But looking back on it now, I can see that he was following the pattern of many young doctors at the time. I had worked to put him through medical school and to set up his practice in Columbus. I loved him and was anxious to build the life we had sacrificed for. The baby was coming and everything looked rosy to me. Then, bam! Adam wanted out."

Charlotte looked sympathetic, and not only to encourage Margot to go on.

"At first I was convinced that there was another woman. I just couldn't believe that Adam simply wanted to move on to another phase of his life—without me, without our baby."

"Has he stayed close to your son?" Charlotte asked.

"Not at all. He's always sent birthday and Christmas presents, but anybody could have picked them out. Even the return addresses on the packages were impersonal—they were always his office address instead of his home address. So I made sure that Charlie sent his thank-you notes to the office. For myself, I haven't written to or talked on the phone with Adam for years."

"Does he ever visit?"

"Almost never. Charlie has seen him only once in the last year, for instance, and that was in June, when he graduated from Wright State.

"When Charlie started college, I wanted to ask Adam to chip in for half of his tuition, but my husband Joe wouldn't hear of it. Said that Charlie was his son all but biologically."

"Sounds like a nice guy. Your husband, I mean."

"Joe's great. We've been married almost fifteen years now. I'm lucky to have him. Of course," Margot said, smiling, "I like to think he's lucky to have me, too."

Charlotte wanted to steer the conversation back to Adam. "It must have been rough, raising a child by yourself. Did Adam's parents help you out?"

"They certainly tried to. But I have an independent streak, and I was determined that Charlie and I would sink or swim on our own. I'm afraid I wasn't very nice to Adam's parents and sister after the divorce."

Margot offered Charlotte more tea and then poured another cup for herself. "That's really the reason I agreed to talk with you. All the Walkers but Adam were decent people, and they weren't responsible for what he did. But I cut myself and Charlie off from them, which I realize now wasn't fair or nice. I regret that, and helping you write a book about them would be a way to atone for having hurt their feelings and deprived them of a grandson."

Charlotte felt a pang of guilt at the mention of the non-existent book. "Your hurt and anger are certainly understandable," she said.

"Perhaps. But I have to be careful not to give you the wrong impression about Adam," Margot said very seriously. "He wasn't an ogre to me. Or, if he was an ogre, he was an awfully polite one. I don't think he ever raised his voice to me, for instance, during the whole time we were married.

"It's just that he saw me primarily as a meal ticket. As a chance to have someone else pay his way through medical school. He was like that. He made plans and didn't let emotions get in the way. Looking back on it, our marriage and our break-up seem very calculated. The lack of involvement that I had always blamed on his studies and long hours at the hospital turned out to be genuine. He *wasn't* very involved with me."

Trying to lighten the atmosphere a little, Charlotte said, "Well, you don't seem to be tortured about him now."

Margot laughed lightly. "My anger at Adam burned out a long time ago. He's simply not worth it, and I've never known *him* to let himself be consumed with emotion—good *or* bad—over another person."

Charlotte realized that Margot's description of Adam's dispassion matched Daphne's description of their marriage. But it didn't square with Daphne's revelation of his involvement with Tiffany.

She pointed out that Adam seemed to be passionate about fine art.

"If he's active in the fine-arts scene in Columbus, then it's the social climbing, not the art that he cares about,"

Margot said. "Unless he's changed dramatically from when I knew him. Then he was only using art as a ticket to the kind of social life he wanted. I think he resented the kind of upbringing he had. It was a loving home, but barely middle class because his father didn't make much as a minister. And then Sarah made sure they didn't accumulate much because she was always giving any extra away to people who were worse off than they were. She was really something. It was obvious that she had the same values that caused her parents to go off and be missionaries. I think she embarrassed Adam."

Margot gave a wry little chuckle.

"I never knew Adam to enjoy a piece of art for itself," she went on. "He was only interested in what it could get for him. Let me give you an example. The only way Mary and George Campbell managed to get themselves and their little Carl safely out of China was to bribe some officials. You already know that from reading their diaries."

"Right," said Charlotte. "I wondered how they got the money for the bribe."

"Oh, they didn't use money," Margot said. "They used a jade necklace that had been given to them by a Chinese family for having saved the life of their sick son."

Charlotte nearly fell off the sofa. Once she recovered, she asked, "They bribed the officials with a jade necklace?"

"Yes, in exchange for safe passage out of Peking. I'm sure the necklace was worth a fortune. Of course, Mary and George saw the hand of God at work in the fact that they had been given the necklace in the first place, so that they would have something to use as a bribe."

"It's too bad that necklace got out of the family," Charlotte said.

"Well, it did and it didn't," Margot said. "Once the Campbells were back in America, there was a great deal of interest in them and their adventure in China. For several months they were besieged for interviews by many different publications, including Methodist Church magazines. The story about the necklace's origin and its use as a bribe seemed to particularly catch people's fancy. The editors of one publication actually hired someone to create a replica of the necklace so that they could photograph it and give their readers a better idea of what the Campbells had used to purchase their lives."

Margot paused. "But I'm probably telling you things you already know, aren't I?"

Stunned at the new information, Charlotte could only shake her head no. Margot smiled and went on.

"Now, why did I start all of this?" she asked. "Oh, yes. I was trying to explain Adam to you.

"The replica necklace was very beautiful, even though it wasn't worth any more than costume jewelry. Sarah gave it to Adam shortly after we were married, and I wore it often while we were together.

"You would have thought that Adam would have treasured that necklace, wouldn't you?" Margot asked. "After all, it represented the one that bought his grandparents' way out of China and there was a good chance Adam's mother and, consequently, Adam himself wouldn't even have been born if it weren't for the original necklace.

"But he didn't have any feeling for it at all, and that's what I'm trying to illustrate for you. The man has no sentimental feelings. The replica was of absolutely no value to him because it had no monetary value. If anybody had offered him even twenty dollars for it, I bet he would have sold it. As it was, I liked it and kept the necklace after we were divorced. Adam couldn't have cared less."

Charlotte was crestfallen. If Margot had the replica, then that couldn't very well be the one Clayton Armstrong had identified as celluloid.

"Could I see it?" Charlotte requested.

"Of course. I'll just be a moment."

Margot was gone much longer than a moment and came back empty-handed. "I'm sorry," she said, seeming puzzled and upset. "I couldn't find it. I haven't worn it for a long time, and I can't imagine how I misplaced it."

But Charlotte was thrilled at the news the replica was

missing. A replica Margot only *thought* she had could be the one Armstrong had tested.

Charlotte tried very hard to keep the excitement out of her voice as she suggested, "Why don't you just describe it to me."

"Well, it's really not all that important," Margot hedged. "As I said, it's only made of celluloid and now I feel silly to have gone on and on about it and then not been able to find it. The only reason I even brought it up was to demonstrate how Adam doesn't get attached to things. Not to me, not to Charlie, not to some old plastic necklace."

"Still, I'd like to know what it looks like."

So Margot described the replica: pale, almost white; four large roundish pieces that had carved dragons, alternating with smaller round pieces that consisted of carved mountains and clouds. Bingo!

Charlotte couldn't resist asking how many claws were on each dragon foot. Margot looked at her as if she thought she had lost her mind.

Just then a tall young man walked into the living room. His resemblance to Adam was striking.

Margot held out her hand to him and said, "Well, hi, Charlie. Get tired of your own cooking and decide to come for Sunday supper?"

Charlie grinned. "You got it," he said, taking his mother's hand.

Margot turned back to Charlotte and made the introductions, adding, "This is the writer from Columbus that I mentioned," for Charlie's benefit.

Charlie stayed only a few minutes before excusing himself, saying he was going to watch a golf match on the TV in the den. Charlotte mentioned the close resemblance of father and son to Margot, who agreed it was there. But, she hastened to add, Charlie didn't *act* a thing like Adam and seemed to have modeled himself after Joe in the personality traits that matter most.

"Sounds like you don't mind that Adam hasn't been around to influence Charlie," Charlotte remarked.

"That's right. About the only thing I've approved of Adam doing in years was his visit here when Charlie graduated."

"Adam was here at the house?"

"Yes. That was the part that was nice for Charlie. Adam attended the graduation ceremony and then came back here. He seemed proud of Charlie and interested in the computer job he expected to get at NCR world headquarters here. He even spent some time talking to Charlie about the Campbell side of the family, which I've never known him to do before.

"Things were going so well between them that Joe and I didn't want to intrude. We went out for some ice cream, and by the time we got back, Adam was ready to leave. I know Charlie thought that maybe his father would want to see more of him after that, but Adam hasn't contacted him since. Which is more typical of him than the nice visit."

"Since Charlie is here," Charlotte said, "would you mind asking him if he knows where the necklace is?"

"He knows where I keep it," Margot said, "but I can't imagine that he would know what's happened to it." Nonetheless, she went out to ask her son to join them for a moment.

"I'd like to show Charlotte the necklace that was made for your great-grandparents when they got back from China, Charlie. Do you know where it is?"

"It's not where you always keep it?"

"No, and I can't find it anywhere."

"You're slipping, Mom," Charlie said. "The last time I looked at it, I put it back in your top bureau drawer."

"You've had it out recently?" she asked him.

"No, not since last year. Graduation night, when Adam was here and you and Joe left for a bit. Remember? Adam was telling me the whole Campbell story and asked me if you still had the celluloid necklace. He asked me to go get it and bring it into the den where we could look at it under the bright light of the desk lamp."

He turned toward Charlotte and said, "There's a fascinating story connected to that old necklace, you know. My mother can tell you all about it."

"She has," Charlotte said, thinking that the young man didn't know the half of it. With a smile, Charlie retreated toward the den.

Charlotte finished up with a few more questions about the Campbells. Then she sincerely thanked Margot for sharing the information about her ex-in-laws and headed out the door, convinced that Margot's replica was safely tucked away in Libby Fox's office and that Adam Walker was the necklace thief.

28

Tuesday

Charlotte was certain she had her necklace thief and a very interesting story to go with it. Two questions remained: Could she get the evidence she needed to demonstrate Adam Walker's guilt? And could she control when the story came out in order to hold on to her exclusive?

She and Lou were in Charlotte's office as she brought Lou up-to-date on her investigation.

"We report to Room oh-one-four at four o'clock tomorrow for our training," Charlotte said.

"All of a sudden, you're saying 'we.' Did I miss something?"

"I need your help, Lou. I've arranged for us to work with Tip-Top Cleaning Services at Riverside Medical Building tomorrow.

"I did miss something. How did Tip-Top Cleaning Services get involved in your investigation?"

"Unknowingly, I assure you. I've never had to lie so much in my life as I have over this necklace business."

Charlotte then explained that she had told the cleaning company's management that she was working on an article about jobs for which college degrees were unnecessary. She was actually performing as many of the jobs as she could for her article, she told the managers. And office cleaning was one she wanted to try out. They had graciously acquiesced to her request to work in Riverside Medical Building.

This would provide a plausible reason for her to gain access to Adam's office. She was virtually certain that if he was the thief, any existing proof for the theft of the necklace would be in his office, rather than at the condo he shared with Daphne. If he had sold the necklace while he and Tiffany were on the West Coast during the weekend after Thanksgiving, he certainly wouldn't want Daphne to know anything about extra money that wouldn't be included in the divorce settlement.

Charlotte was not brave enough to check out Adam's office by herself. Asking Walt to help was out of the question, given his general instincts to rule out breaking and entering. But she figured Lou would be game. And the description of their masquerading as cleaning ladies in pursuit of evidence would lend a nice touch to her necklace articles.

"Maybe I'll do some cleaning at home tonight to get in shape," Lou said, after agreeing to help Charlotte. "I think I'll look for a bandanna to wear on my head."

"I can always count on you for the important things."

They reported to Room 014 at four o'clock the next afternoon. They were wearing baggy old pants, work shirts, and running shoes. And bandannas. Each was carrying a notebook to record her observations.

Joan Turpin, the Tip-Top supervisor, was there to provide their training. She was pleased that someone was going to write about office-cleaning services. Her indignation about her line of work being listed in the yellow pages as "Janitorial Services" was heartfelt.

The training was brief and centered on the safety aspects of the job. Lou and Charlotte were given rubber gloves and told to wear them at all times when they were dealing with medical waste. All the wastebaskets in the doctors' offices and the examining rooms had red plastic liners that were to be closed with plastic ties and put into the large red containers, marked "Medical Waste," that would be in the halls. New red plastic liners were then to be placed in the wastebaskets.

When Joan asked Charlotte and Lou if they had any preference for which floor they'd like to work on, they chorused, "The first," knowing that was where Adam's office was located. Joan nodded, saying, "Good choice. You'll get a chance at a variety of things—lobby, offices, rest rooms."

Joan took them down to the end of a corridor and supervised their work through two sets of offices. Satisfied that they were being careful with the medical waste, she gave them the keys for the corridor and went off to check on her other workers.

Charlotte and Lou worked their way to Walker's office suite. Having been there before, Charlotte vaguely knew the plastic surgeon's layout: waiting room, receptionist's office, and, off an interior corridor, she supposed, examining rooms and the doctor's office.

"How much do you think he pays for this?" Lou whispered.

"Think about how much people pay for procedures that have more to do with vanity than health," Charlotte responded. "Why are we whispering?"

Shrugging, Lou closed the door from the suite entrance to the main corridor and asked in a normal tone, "Should we lock this?"

"Let's not," Charlotte decided. "We'll be able to hear Joan if she comes in. Anyway, we'll be behind at least one more door while we're searching. You look in Tiffany's area while I empty the wastebaskets. Then I'll search the back rooms while you're the lookout in the reception area."

Lou agreed and went into Tiffany's office, while Charlotte put on her rubber gloves and collected the trash, bringing it into the reception area.

Lou soon came into the waiting room. "Five big cabinets of files in there, and they're all locked."

"They're probably just patient files. Doctors always keep those under lock and key. I'll go see what's in Adam's office."

There was nothing on his desk except an ivory-colored Touch-Tone telephone and a fancy Rolodex. No personal items. No family pictures. And the desk was locked.

Charlotte checked quickly through the bookshelves for anything that looked suspicious, but turned up nothing. There was a locked, glass-fronted wall cabinet containing various medical supplies and drugs. Unless the genuine necklace was stuffed into a roll of cotton, there was nothing of interest there.

Glad her fingerprints were covered by the rubber gloves, Charlotte then went through the Rolodex. Lots of other doctors, a lawyer, the car dealer where he'd gotten his Lamborghini, and several up-scale restaurants were listed.

Interestingly, Richard Ransom was in the file. On the card for Ransom, two phone numbers, both with out-of-state area codes, were penciled in, in addition to Ransom's Columbus number. Charlotte copied the numbers into her notebook.

She remembered that when she'd misplaced the key for her desk at the office, the maintenance supervisor had asked for the number on the lock in order to get a duplicate. So she also copied the number on Adam's desk lock into her notebook.

She was about to leave Adam's office when she heard Lou say loudly, "Why, hello, Doctor." She stopped dead, immediately recognizing Adam's voice as he said, "No reason to stop your work. I'm just here to pick up something. I'll only be a minute."

Terrified, Charlotte slipped behind the open door to his office, pressing as flat as she could against the wall and trying not to breathe, at least not audibly. Adam entered the office and then took what seemed like forever to Charlotte to scan his bookshelves and make his selection. She prayed that he not find it necessary to close his door. He didn't and left.

And then Charlotte nearly hyperventilated. She managed

to get herself under control and went out to the reception area, where she found Lou wielding the vacuum cleaner in an adrenaline frenzy. They agreed to hold off all discussion until they were out of the building.

As they were leaving Adam's suite with the plastic bags of trash, Joan came by to ask how they were doing on their project. They both jumped, then realized she meant job research—not necklace-theft investigation.

"We should probably come back at least one more night," Charlotte said, "just to be sure that we haven't missed out on anything that should be included in the article. Tomorrow night okay?"

Joan agreed and sent them on to clean the women's rest room. Muttering under her breath, Charlotte tackled the toilets. "It was Melanie who got me into all this," she grumped.

"Just think of it as hands-on research," Lou returned.

Afterward, they drove separately to Lou's house. While Lou was microwaving popcorn, Charlotte checked out her friend's progress with a five-thousand piece jigsaw puzzle of a Brueghel painting.

The reddish-orange (burnt sienna, if you had the big box of crayons) puzzle pieces that Lou had sorted out earlier seemed to be going together nicely to form one of the hundred proverbs that Brueghel had included in the picture. Evidently in his day, "Pie in the sky" had been "Pie on the roof."

"I see you've put together 'Walls have ears,' " Charlotte remarked.

"That's why I didn't want to talk over at Riverside. You never know who might be around. Including your suspect, obviously."

"Breaking and entering really does make you paranoid, doesn't it?" Charlotte said.

"We weren't really breaking and entering," Lou responded a little defensively. "We had a legitimate right to be there."

"We had the right to be there to clean," Charlotte reminded her.

They sat at Lou's kitchen table with a big bowl of popcorn between them.

"Well"—Lou shrugged—"as we used to say in grad school, sometimes paranoia is the result of people trying to get you. So what should we do now?"

"Let's find out what the phone numbers get us," Charlotte suggested.

Using the white pages, they ascertained that the 213 number was in the Los Angeles area, while the 201 number was in northern New Jersey.

They tried the New Jersey number first, but a recording told them it had been disconnected.

"Los Angeles. That's where Tiffany told you that she and Adam had spent Thanksgiving, wasn't it?" asked Lou. Charlotte nodded.

"Okay, let's try that number," Lou said, dialing. After four rings, a recording came on that said she had reached Chan's Import-Export Shop and gave its business hours.

She relayed this information to Charlotte. "Interesting. I wonder what they import. More important, I wonder if they export stolen art."

"Maybe Chan is one of those crooked dealers that Richard Ransom told you about," Lou said. "After all, it was Ransom's Rolodex card that these numbers were on."

"That's right."

"You don't suppose Adam and he are in this together, do you? Maybe he promised Ransom a percentage of the sale in return for information on crooked art dealers," Lou suggested.

"Why would Adam bring anyone in on the sale of the jade necklace? I think he'd have wanted all the money he could get to fund his new life with Tiffany."

"Is that woman's intuition or logic?"

"Both," Charlotte answered. They laughed and discussed how they would call Joan Turpin the next evening if Charlotte wasn't able to get a copy of the key to Walker's desk by then. There was no point in a return visit until they could penetrate his inner sanctum.

Thursday

Charlotte had no difficulty getting a copy of the key, and she and Lou met with Joan Turpin again briefly at four-thirty.

For variety, they started with the lobby, then worked back on down the corridor. Joan had unlocked the first suite of offices for them, then handed them the keys. Charlotte and Lou zipped through the first four suites.

Then it was time for Adam's office. This time, Charlotte locked the door behind them. She knew it wouldn't keep Adam out if he returned, but the sound of his key in the lock would alert them.

Charlotte immediately tested the duplicate desk key. It worked easily. The center drawer had the usual pencils, pens, paper clips, and other miscellany, along with Adam's prescription pads. Of course, that would be why he kept it locked, thought Charlotte, disappointed. Maybe there won't be anything interesting here, after all.

She tried the deep drawer on the right side of the desk. It contained a number of unmarked file folders. She lifted them out and started thumbing through them.

The files appeared to be primarily for bills and receipts— one for the Lamborghini, one for jewelry (Charlotte wondered if it was for Daphne or Tiffany), one for sports equipment, et cetera, et cetera. There was one folder that contained receipts going back to 1968. Most of them were from toy stores and were from July and December of nearly every year. It took a few moments' thought, but Charlotte finally surmised that the receipts were for presents for Charlie Walker at Christmas and, she supposed, his birthday.

The last file folder yielded a single sheet of paper. The letterhead at the top was from a Swiss bank. Eight numbers, with dashes between each number, were handwritten on the stationary.

Well, I'll be damned, she thought. A Swiss bank account. Just like in the Ludlum books. Nobody will ever be able to get information about that—certainly not the police. I bet that's where the money from the necklace is stashed.

She quickly removed the rubber glove from her right hand, got her notebook and pencil out of her shirt pocket, and jotted down the information from the letterhead and the numbers.

She put the glove back on, meticulously returned the files to the desk drawer, and locked the desk. The notebook, pencil, and desk key went back into her shirt pocket.

She and Lou were finished with their stint as office cleaners.

29

"B ut I don't work for the police, Lou," Charlotte insisted. "I'm a writer and it's my job to get information out about the stolen necklace and who stole it. It's not my job to actually help the police arrest Adam."

"But you went to Barnes before."

"For protection. And you saw what good it did me, too."

Lou—suddenly afflicted with public-spiritedness, now that her stint as a criminal was over—had been trying for some time to convince Charlotte she should go to the police with everything she knew about the necklace and Walker. They were sitting at Lou's kitchen table after their second visit to Adam's office.

"In the first place, we're only talking about theft. It's not as though I'm letting a murderer roam the streets without telling the police."

"No, it's Barry Abrams you're planning to finger for murder," Lou accused her.

"But I don't have enough evidence for that. And I never will if I start working for the police. Every time journalists cooperate with the cops, their sources dry up because people stop trusting them. And rightfully so, I might add."

"I think you're just protecting your exclusive," Lou argued. "You don't want anyone else—even the police—to find out about the stolen necklace until you can write your precious stories."

"Well, I never noticed you letting any other researchers publish the results of your studies, either," Charlotte stated, pleased to see that Lou had no answer to that. Furthermore, she knew all her evidence was circumstantial at best: Adam's trip to Seattle, Margot's replica necklace's disappearance after his visit, the phone number for Chan's, and the number of a Swiss bank account. What she needed was something more conclusive.

"Can you think of any way that we could get Adam to actually confess?" she asked.

"Not unless we kidnap Tiffany and demand a confession as the ransom."

"Wow, talk about a career ladder . . . Twenty minutes ago you were only breaking and entering. Now you're suggesting a capital crime."

Lou laughed.

Suddenly Charlotte had the answer. They *would* commit a crime. They'd blackmail Adam, saying that if he didn't pay they'd go to the police with their evidence. If he paid or threatened them, that would be as good as a confession of guilt for stealing the necklace. Quickly, she outlined the plan for Lou.

"You've taken leave of your senses, Charlotte," Lou said incredulously. "Of all the harebrained—"

"I think it's just crazy enough to work."

"You're conveniently overlooking the fact that blackmail is illegal."

"You didn't think it was illegal for me to open his desk?"

"I understood what we were doing. But this seems so much worse."

"Semantics," Charlotte said dismissively. "Like it or not, we're in this up to our eyeballs. The only question is whether we have the guts to complete what we set out to do—nail the necklace thief. Don't lose heart now, just when we're about to expose him."

"The only thing I volunteered for at the Son of Heaven

exhibit was to guide groups of students through the show," Lou protested. "I didn't bargain for breaking and entering and blackmail and who knows what else you're going to suggest next. Besides, it sounds dangerous."

"It doesn't have to be," Charlotte insisted. "In the first place, he's just a thief. I don't think he had anything to do with Phil's death. Maybe nobody did, if you can believe Detective Barnes and the heart-attack finding. In the second place, we can design our blackmail scheme so that it's as safe as possible. We'll have him give us the money in a very public place so that he can't try anything funny. And if he is as dispassionate as both Margot and Daphne say, that's not very likely anyway."

"What will you do with the blackmail money?" Lou asked, and Charlotte sensed her friend was getting interested in spite of herself.

"I'll just hold it as evidence to back up my story until Walker is eventually arrested," Charlotte answered.

Lou said, "I'd feel better if you took it to the police."

"Not until after he's arrested," Charlotte responded. "In the meantime, I'll just keep it in the bank."

"In a separate account," Lou insisted.

Charlotte agreed and the deal was on.

As Charlotte paced around the kitchen, they decided that a phone call indicating knowlege of the Swiss bank account would be the information most likely to get a response from Walker. They discussed various amounts of money to ask for, ranging from $1,000 to $100,000, and settled on $10,000 as a non-trivial amount that he could probably come up with fairly quickly.

Charlotte suggested they have him deliver the money during intermission at jazz singer Diane Schuur's show at the Ohio Theatre the following Saturday night. She and Walt, and Lou, already had tickets.

Lou concurred, saying, "That's a good idea. That's one of the most public places in town and I'm sure we can still get a ticket and send it to him. Or better yet, we could have it delivered to his office. Maybe we could send him a singing telegram, with the ticket in a gift envelope."

Amazed at her friend's sudden enthusiasm for the task, Charlotte said, "That's a nice touch. Let's—"

"Wait," Lou interrupted. "You know Walt's not going to want you to be involved in this, Charlotte. Maybe we better think of another drop-off time and place."

"Oh, come on, Lou. Old married couples don't tell each other everything. I won't breathe a word of this to Walt. He probably wouldn't believe me if I did. Besides, we don't even know yet if Adam will take the bait."

"That's true. Also, we'll need to give him some time to get the money together."

"If we call him tonight, that would give him only one banking day before the show. Think that's enough?"

"I'm sure he and Daphne probably have ten grand lying around the house," Lou remarked dryly.

"If we're going to remain anonymous, you're going to have to be the one to call him and to meet him for the payment at the theater, Lou. Since I interviewed him, he'd be sure to recognize me."

"But he's seen me, too. When he barged in on our cleaning, remember?"

"You were wearing a bandanna at the time. I am happy to say that you looked nothing like your real self in that getup. Besides, no one ever really *sees* a cleaning lady."

In a couple of minutes, they were deep in the development of a phone script. It was just after eight when Lou dialed the Walkers' number. After several rings, a firm voice said, "Dr. Walker speaking."

Lou immediately began reading the script. "Dr. Walker, I'm going to read you some statistics. I don't want you to respond until I have finished the whole list. First, five claws. Second, nine dragons. Third, one fake jade necklace. Fourth, one trip to Seattle and Los Angeles. Fifth, area code 213-555-9191. Sixth, 0-12-17-7-0-6-26-0."

"What do you want?" whispered Adam, his voice obviously shaky.

"Ten thousand dollars in used one-hundred-dollar bills. Be sure that the serial numbers aren't in order. Get the money tomorrow. We'll let you know where to deliver it and when. And don't say anything about this to anybody or we'll go to the cops." Lou cut the connection abruptly.

Then she let out a cheer. "He bought it. I'm sure of it."

An exuberant Charlotte replied, "I feel like we've won already. The secret to everything was separating the necklace investigation from the murder investigation. Once we get Adam to confess, I can go back to investigating Phil's death. This is going to be an incredible story."

"One step at a time, Charlotte. Let's not count our criminals until they are incriminated."

"You're right, of course. Let me know how you do with Walker's ticket."

Before going home, Charlotte stopped in the electronics store on West Lane Avenue. She explained to a saleswoman what she needed.

"We read plays," Charlotte said. "We don't act them out completely, but we do try to move around according to the stage directions. We were hoping to find body microphones that could be hooked up with tape recorders so that we could tape our performances. Is that possible?"

"Actually," said the clerk, "the mike wouldn't need to be hooked up to the tape recorder. We have very small tape recorders with built-in microphones that do a pretty good job of recording any voices, noises, what have you, for a distance of thirty feet."

Friday

Lou called the next evening to report on her success with the ticket for Adam for the Saturday-night show.

"I was able to get one on the aisle," she said, "in the next section over from us in the loge. They'd had a return just before I got to the box office. Then I wrote up the instructions we'd agreed on, sealed them in the ticket envelope, and went to that balloon place at Sixteenth and High. They delivered the envelope this afternoon with a bunch of balloons and sang 'For He's a Jolly Good Fellow.' I thought that was appropriate for the occasion."

"Sounds good, Lou," Charlotte said blandly. "Walt and I are really looking forward to Saturday night."

Realizing that Charlotte's tone meant Walt was nearby, Lou said, "Got you. Incidentally, I found the recorder you left for me in the mailbox. Sorry I wasn't here to receive it personally. I'll see you tomorrow. Bye."

Perfect, Charlotte thought, hanging up. Everything was falling into place.

She and Walt spent most of the evening trying to teach Tyler and Kevin the rudiments of contract bridge. Later, after the boys had trooped over to Kevin's house to spend the night, Walt and Charlotte still sat at the card table set up in the living room. Walt mentioned that she had seemed absentminded during their card playing.

"I do realize," he said, chuckling, "that it was difficult to follow the bidding when the boys insisted on 'rapping' their bids. But you seemed to have trouble concentrating."

Knowing full well that her mind had been on the blackmail payment scheduled for the next evening, Charlotte mumbled something about just being tired.

"It's all this work you've been doing for the necklace article," Walt said. "I'll be glad when the show's over and you can stop investigating and finally start writing. Then you can get back to normal."

Charlotte smiled, knowing she would be back to normal far sooner than Walt thought: in about twenty-four hours, if Walker brought the blackmail payment as his virtual confession.

She had told Walt about her interview with Margot Paretsky, but hadn't mentioned masquerading as a cleaning lady or her new career in blackmail. Such shenanigans would make him think she'd lost her mind. Besides, since he had not believed the driver of the blue car had deliberately attempted to run her down, why should she think he'd believe that a wealthy and successful plastic surgeon could be stealing works of art? Or at least *a* work of art and its plastic replica.

Hoping to avoid any discussion that could lead to her spilling the beans about the next evening's activities, Charlotte got up from the card table, put the bridge decks in a drawer, and suggested they turn in.

But Walt moved to the couch, his mind still on the necklace article. Charlotte sat down next to him.

"I've been thinking about your certainty that Adam Walker stole the fake necklace from Margot and switched it for the real one in the show," he said. "How come you're so sure that Margot herself didn't switch the necklaces?"

Because Walker responded to our blackmail demand, Charlotte thought confidently, saying nothing.

"After all," Walt continued, "she was the last person you know of who had possession of the fake."

Charlotte asked what Margot's motive for switching the necklaces could have been.

"Like anyone else, she could have wanted the money she'd get from selling the real one. Or maybe," Walt said, warming to the idea, "her motive was revenge. Maybe she wanted to frame her ex-husband, who had treated her and their son so cruelly."

Charlotte looked at him quizzically.

"In which case," he went on, "her scheme has worked beautifully, because you are absolutely convinced Adam is the necklace thief."

"That's right, I am," Charlotte said mildly. "But I think you're forgetting that Margot didn't have a thing to do with my finding her. I located her all by myself—and with considerable resourcefulness, I might add. She couldn't have planned to frame Adam through me or my article."

"Of course not. You're the unexpected player in this

whole thing. You simply stumbled into it after Phil declared there was a fake in the show."

"Thank you for emphasizing the grace with which I do my job."

"Sorry. But you know what I mean. You didn't set out to look for a fake in the Son of Heaven show. And Margot wouldn't have needed you in order to set up Adam. For all you know, it could have been Margot who alerted Phil to the fake in the first place."

"I don't have reason to think *anybody* alerted Phil to the fake. I think his art history scholarship resulted in its identification."

"But why would he have concentrated on that particular necklace? An anonymous phone call from Margot would have been enough to make him check it out the night of the show's opening dinner. And Margot would have known that once the fake was discovered, it could be traced to the Walker family."

Walt seemed inordinately pleased with his conjecture, Charlotte thought, becoming a little annoyed with his attitude. Without having done any of the work she had, he considered his guess to be as good as her careful weighing of the evidence. Of course, there was evidence that he didn't know about.

"Margot made sure she told you about Adam's connection with the necklace, didn't she?" Walt persisted.

"I had to pry that information out of her," Charlotte said, trying to remember whether that was really true. "Your ideas are all very clever, except that Margot didn't seem to want revenge. They've been divorced for over twenty years now, and I'm sure the anger she felt when he left her has disappeared. She said as much, in fact."

"But you have to admit she makes a great suspect."

"To tell you the truth, Walt, sometimes *everybody* looks like a great suspect to me," Charlotte said wearily.

30

Saturday

It was Saturday evening, April Fool's Day, and the aptness of the date was not lost on Charlotte. By this time, the scheme she and Lou had concocted to force an incriminating payoff from Adam Walker seemed a bit insane. Bizarre. Ludicrous. Most of all, Charlotte was embarrassed to realize, it seemed like something Lucy Ricardo and Ethel Mertz would have cooked up behind Ricky's back.

Nervously, she dressed to go hear Diane Schuur perform at the Ohio Theatre. She slipped on the antique jade necklace she had worn to the Son of Heaven gala that had started all this necklace-theft business a month ago, thinking that wearing it added a certain symmetry.

Walt parked in the lot under the State House across the street from the Ohio Theatre. The lot, with its very low ceiling and vast, dim space, had never seemed more cavernous to Charlotte. She was relieved when they reached the top of the stairs and walked out into the night air at High and State streets. The Ohio's blazing marquee looked festive and safe across the street. DIANE SCHUUR—IN CONCERT was spelled out in lights. "Special Attraction at Intermission," Charlotte added to herself.

The Ohio Theatre was built in 1928 as a Loew's movie theater, having been designed by Thomas Lamb, who was designing entertainment palaces all over America. The Ohio

Theatre was palatial, all right. It was full of lush carpeting; Chinese silk wall panels; wide, sweeping marble staircases; extensive brass and bronze trim; and lots of rococo plaster-work. The 300-light crystal chandelier was enormous.

Attached to the east side of the theater building was the Galbreath Pavilion, a three-story glass-and-marble addition where theatergoers were served refreshments. Only a door separated the third floor of the pavilion from the loge and the balcony.

As she and Walt entered the theater, Charlotte was re-assured by the large crowd drawn by Schuur's performance. She and Lou had chosen this as the site for Adam's blackmail payoff because they felt its very public nature afforded them the best security. The thief couldn't very well try anything funny in front of the hundreds of people who would be milling around the pavilion during intermission.

Their seats were in the loge, and Charlotte's phobia of high open spaces forced her to hesitate as they came into that area from the west side of the theater. She could see the proscenium, orchestra pit, some orchestra-section seats, and the loge seats below her on her right. To her left, the balcony stretched up seemingly forever. She got her bear-ings, gritted her teeth, and concentrated on Walt's back as he preceded her down the aisle to their seats.

Lou was already seated and waiting for them. Walt stood aside to let Charlotte enter the row first so that she could sit next to her friend.

Once seated, Charlotte tilted her head back to look for the brass flying horses that hung amid the crystal gewgaws on the chandelier. Legend had it that when the chandelier was completed, someone had complained to the theater de-signer that he had hung "everything but flying horses" on it. Gleefully, he added the brass horses. Now Charlotte smiled, as she always did, at the horses' incongruity with the rest of the formal chandelier.

Lou was wearing a long red tunic with deep pockets over a white turtleneck sweater and dark slacks. When she noticed Charlotte staring at the pockets, she smiled and gently patted the right one, indicating the whereabouts of the tiny tape recorder. Charlotte assumed that the larger-than-usual purse at Lou's feet would hold the ten thousand dollars that Adam was bringing them.

Speaking of Adam—where was the good doctor? Charlotte turned around in her seat and casually let her eyes roam behind and above. She spotted the seat for which they had sent him a ticket. It was empty.

Only ten more minutes to show time. Would Adam show up? Charlotte saw Lou glancing furtively toward Adam's seat and correctly assumed that it was Adam's entrance into the loge that suddenly caused her friend to jerk her gaze away and face forward. She elbowed Lou and grinned.

The curtain went up with an orchestral flourish, and the performance began. Despite their extracurricular plans for intermission, Charlotte and Lou enjoyed the show. Walt seemed to also, but then, he didn't have their reason to be distracted.

Schuur's four-octave voice moved skillfully through bigband and blues tunes, backed by the Columbus Jazz Arts Group. The crowd was entranced with her expertise with songs such as "Easy to Love," "Everyday I Have the Blues," and "Travelin' Light." Intermission seemed to come awfully soon.

The plan was, that during intermission, Lou would go out into the pavilion off the loge and find Adam. Charlotte would tell Walt she was going to the rest room, and follow a few moments later to watch the encounter surreptitiously—just in case Lou should need her assistance.

The instructions they had sent Adam with the ticket had spelled out that he would be able to identify Lou because she would be wearing a red tunic and an "Ohio: The Heart of It All" tourism button. (She and Charlotte had settled on the button because they could be certain that no one else at the elegant Ohio Theatre would be wearing such a tacky accessory.)

Intermission. As Lou excused herself to Walt and Charlotte and walked across the loge toward the pavilion, Charlotte noticed that she wasn't wearing the button. She tried unsuccessfully to catch Lou's attention, but to no avail.

Lou was totally aware she was not wearing the button. She had not yet put it on because she had decided that she wanted to observe Adam for a little while, without his being able to recognize her from the button.

She was not much worried that he would hurt her. How could he, with all these people around? But she was concerned that she would somehow mess things up and fail to get Adam's confession or the incriminating payoff.

As Lou walked from the loge into the crowded pavilion, she became concerned that she and Charlotte had chosen *too* public a place for the encounter with Adam. There were so many people standing around chatting and sipping their wine that she couldn't spot him. She was beginning to worry whether she would find him in the crowd before the fifteen-minute intermission was over.

Finally, she found him. He was standing drinking a glass of wine at the south end of the pavilion, with his back to the glass wall. He was alone, although she saw him nod at a couple as they passed him.

The elevators that operated between the three floors of the pavilion were nearby, and it occured to Lou that Adam would flee out those elevators once he handed over the money to her. She reached into her right pocket and turned on the tape recorder.

Trying to appear confident, she approached Adam and spoke his name. As he turned toward her, she drew out the tourism button, showed it to him in the palm of her hand, and placed it back in her left tunic pocket.

"I think you're waiting for me," she said. The doctor's handsome face remained impassive; his blue eyes looked at her coldly.

"Let's get this over with," he said. "I'll be more comfortable if we move back here out of the way a bit." He gestured toward the end of the corridor, near the elevators.

Lou didn't hesitate to follow him. She didn't care if he made a quick exit—*after* he had turned over the money.

Back in the loge, it was time for Charlotte to go to the rest room, but actually to find Lou. She was about to leave her seat when the fire alarm suddenly went off shrilly. Charlotte and Walt and everybody else looked at one another, as people always do in these situations, while they waited for the announcement over the loudspeaker that the alarm should be ignored.

But no announcement came, and it seemed to dawn on the crowd collectively that the sixty-one-year-old Ohio Theatre could go up in smoke. There was instant pandemonium as people desperately tried to leave the theater. Walt grabbed Charlotte's hand and they headed for the nearest exit along with everybody else in the loge and balcony.

Inside the west stairwell, Charlotte and Walt were engulfed by the jostling tide of concertgoers urgently making their way to the ground floor and safety outside. The fire alarm clanged incessantly as the crowd alternately surged ahead and stopped, surged ahead and stopped. Charlotte would have held her hands over her ears, but Walt still held one hand in a determined grip, as though he was worried he might lose her in the crowd.

She wondered whether Lou would reach the ground floor before they did and where the three of them would convene outside. She cursed under her breath. If the Ohio was going to catch fire, why did it have to happen during the blackmail payoff?

It seemed to take forever for them to reach the ground floor, but it had actually been only about five minutes. Now they could make no further progress until the gridlock of people formed at the front doors cleared out.

Charlotte and Walt were stalled next to a wall poster for the Columbus Light Opera's upcoming performance of *Cyrano de Bergerac*. Cyrano's exaggerated nose took up most of the colorful poster and made Charlotte recall the words of the threatening phone call she had received: "People who stick their noses in where they don't belong sometimes get them cut off."

What an odd threat, she thought again. She remembered telling Detective Barnes that today's teenagers would never say such a thing. Once she had this necklace-theft story wrapped up, she'd be able to concentrate on Phil's death again. Then she'd try to figure out who would be likely to make that particular threat.

As they waited, Walt nodded toward Cyrano in the poster and said, "That man needs a plastic surgeon—bad."

Charlotte stared at her husband, her eyes growing wide with horror as she realized what she had done.

How could she have been so stupid? It seemed so obvious now. Who would have made such a threat? Someone who specialized in noses, of course. A plastic surgeon like the one she had sent Lou to meet upstairs. It all flooded over her in an instant.

Adam wasn't just the necklace thief; he was the murderer. The two crimes had been connected after all. He had murdered Phil to cover up his theft of the necklace. Barry Abrams probably just had the bad luck of loving Melanie. When two things occured together, one wasn't always the cause of the other. But *sometimes* it was.

Her mind raced. What if Adam had set the theater on fire to kill Lou? Or what if there had never been a fire in the theater, but Adam had set off the alarm to empty the building so he could kill Lou without being seen?

She turned toward Walt and shouted over the noise of the crowd around them, "I'm going back up to find Lou!"

"No! We'll find her outside!"

Charlotte knew that if she went outside the theater, the firefighters who were on their way would never let her back in. There wasn't time to explain to Walt what was happening. Besides, what could she say? Walt, Lou's going to be killed up in the pavilion by the plastic surgeon that we've blackmailed for stealing the necklace, and incidentally, I've just realized that he's also the man who murdered Phil?

Charlotte broke Walt's grip on her hand, turned around, and started pushing her way across the lobby and up the stairway in the pavilion. She could hear Walt calling her name behind her. Glancing down at the lobby from halfway up the stairs, she saw him struggling to follow her. But he had been caught by a new current of people pouring into the lobby from orchestra seats and wasn't making much headway.

There were more people still coming down these stairs than were left on the ones across the theater that she and Walt had used. Perhaps, Charlotte thought, that was because when the alarm went off there were more people having refreshments in the pavilion than were in the loge and balcony. She hoped that the stream of people still extended to the third floor so that Lou was not up there all alone with a killer.

It was hard bucking the tide coming down the stairs. By the time she reached the second-floor landing, Charlotte was no longer trying to avoid elbowing and stepping on the feet of those who were slow to move aside when she told them to let her by. There simply wasn't time for niceties when her friend's life might be at risk.

The crowd thinned out dramatically beyond the second floor, and Charlotte could move much quicker. The noise of the theatergoers seemed faint below her and the fire alarm had stopped. By the time she reached the top, the stairs were deserted. In the dim light coming only from the exit signs and from outside through the glass walls, she stumbled against something. It was Lou's large purse.

"Lou!" she cried. There was no answer. Where could she be?

The rotating lights from emergency vehicles arriving outside could be seen even here on the third floor. The lights made odd patterns on the far walls of the pavilion. Charlotte cautiously walked toward the loge, uncomfortable in the large empty space. She prayed that she would not be too late.

Without the glass walls, the loge was even darker than the pavilion when she opened the door. As she stood still a moment to get her bearings, she heard scuffling to her left, down toward the front of the loge. She could make out two shapes swaying together at the railing over the orchestra seats and immediately knew that they were Lou and Walker. As they grappled at the railing, Adam seemed to tower over the shorter Lou.

"Stop! Let her go!" Charlotte screamed at him. But there was no response from either swaying shape below, no indication they knew she was there. Walker would succeed in killing Lou unless she went down to the front of the loge and stopped him herself. But she wasn't sure she could make herself go down there. She was terrified of the immense open space in front of her, seemingly boundless over the loge seats and the orchestra seats below them. The stage looked smaller than she had ever remembered seeing it, as though it were fathoms below. Without being able to concentrate on Walt's back preceding her down the aisle as she had earlier in the evening, she knew she would feel as if she would float off into space at the top of the theater. Up around the flying horses. Heights, how she hated them.

She had no choice. She moved down the carpeted steps, hanging on to seat backs next to the aisle. She tried to keep her eyes on the carpet and the seat she was holding on to so that she would not be paralyzed by her fear. Moving down the steps took all of her concentration and she did not even think of calling out to Adam again until she reached the aisle that ran between the first row of seats and the railing.

He had Lou backed up against the railing. She was bent backward at the waist, with her shoulders over the railing, and Adam was struggling to push her completely over. His hands were wrapped around Lou's neck. But Lou had anchored herself by wrapping her legs around his and he was not yet able to get her over. One of Lou's hands was pressing weakly against Adam's chest and the other pried unsuccessfully at his fingers around her neck. Tilting her completely over the railing would not be difficult once Lou lost consciousness.

Without thinking, Charlotte lunged at the struggling pair. As she connected with him, Adam let go of Lou's neck with one hand and swung a side-armed blow at Charlotte. His forearm hit her square in the forehead and knocked her backward onto the floor. Her hip landed on something sharp, hurting more than her head. It was Lou's tourism button that had fallen out of her pocket during her struggle with Adam.

Charlotte grabbed the button as she got up and quickly bent the shaft of the pin out straight. The flat metal button part would give her something to hold on to. Thus armed, she flew at Adam, who had seemed to redouble his efforts to hoist Lou over the railing. Again and again she plunged the button's pin into Adam's neck and cheek and one hand, the one wrapped around Lou's neck. Finally, he was forced to release Lou and deal with Charlotte. Her elation at freeing Lou was short-lived as Lou released her leg grip on Adam and slipped to the floor in a heap.

With both his hands free, Adam had only to catch and hold Charlotte's button-wielding hand in order to defuse the "weapon's" effectiveness. They wrestled for a moment, his height and superior upper-body strength clearly giving him the advantage.

But it was too early to count Lou out. As Charlotte and Adam grappled above her, she crawled over and wrapped her arms around one of Adam's legs and pulled his foot out from under him. Adam and Charlotte both toppled to the floor. Charlotte untangled herself and sat on his chest. Lou held on to his feet and legs.

As the three of them panted with their exertions, Charlotte looked down at the incapacitated plastic surgeon. One side of his handsome face was covered with bloody pinpricks and scratches. Those cold blue eyes stared back at her with recognition. He knew who she was.

It wasn't long until the firefighters and Walt burst through the loge door above them.

EPILOGUE

When Adam Walker was arrested and charged with the assault on and attempted murder of Lou Toreson, Tiffany Shore quit her job and moved out of state. She left no forwarding address.

In the weeks that followed, the police confirmed that the delivery label on Charlotte's broken figurine had been typed on Adam's typewriter. Joan Turpin's Tip-Top cleaning crew told them that Adam had not been in his office the night Stevenson was killed—doing case notes or anything else.

The police were also able to confirm that Adam's Lamborghini had not left the Waterford garage that evening. The guard remembered that the car had sat under the eye of the video camera in the garage the whole evening of the ice storm. It must have been a short but slippery walk from the Waterford to Columbus Central that night.

Confronted with all this evidence, Adam confessed to stealing the replica necklace from Margot, stealing the jade necklace from the Son of Heaven show and substituting Margot's, murdering an exhibit guard in Seattle, and, finally, murdering Phil Stevenson in Columbus.

Stevenson's and the Seattle guard's heart attacks had been caused by pressure on the vagus nerve in the neck, with which Adam, with all his experience with face-lifts and chin tucks, was all too familiar.

Lou explained that Adam had also tried the vagus nerve technique on her at the theater. She said that she hadn't known why he had clamped his hand to the side of her face and neck as he handed her the envelope filled with the blackmail money. But she knew he was up to no good. She had grabbed his hand and, as they struggled, she used her other hand to pull the fire alarm on the wall behind her near the pavilion elevators, in an attempt to summon help.

Of course, the alarm had worked in the reverse. It had sent people away from the elevators, scurrying down the steps and out of the building. The enterprising Adam had come up with a new plan: he'd drag Lou through the doors separating the pavilion from the loge and down to the railing above the orchestra seats. Then he'd send her over the railing, plunging her to her death thirty feet below.

Daphne Walker was utterly amazed to learn of the existence of Charlie Walker. Her father probably would have been unable to obtain the Church annulment of Adam's first marriage had the Church known about the child. Her lawyers told her there was no question she would get the divorce settlement she wanted.

Detective Jefferson Barnes decided that no charges of breaking and entering or blackmail were necessary. He told Charlotte that he had found it more than coincidental that both she and Phil Stevenson had received metallic-voiced phone calls. (Phil's department's secretary had supplied the information about Phil's call when the police interviewed her about his death.) But the coroner's report had indicated Phil was not murdered, so Barnes chose not to alarm Charlotte further by mentioning Phil's similiar call when she reported her own. Nonetheless, he had assigned officers in cruisers to do casual surveillance when they were in her area, feeling that perhaps the police owed her at least that cursory protection.

No evidence became available to link Adam Walker with the blue car incident, and Charlotte never learned any more about it. Walt was nice enough to avoid saying "I told you so," but Charlotte was convinced Walker had been behind it.

The necklace replica, labeled as such, was taken from its exile in Libby Fox's office and quietly returned to the exhibit. Unfortunately, Charlotte was not the first to break the story of the replica in the local media. But contrary to what Libby had feared, crowds at Son of Heaven increased dramatically as people rolled in to see "the famous fake." The exhibit had its 275,000th visitor on May 25, which put attendance well ahead of the early projections. Once the show closed, the replica would be returned to Margot Paretsky. The FBI were searching for the genuine jade necklace.

Richard Ransom told Charlotte that the reason he had lied about the Alliance Insurance coverage was that he thought she was mixed up in the necklace substitution. He seemed embarrassed to have suspected her while he unknowingly aided the real thief.

Sigrid Olsen soon accepted the directorship of the city's Recreation and Parks Department, saying that her work with Son of Heaven had convinced her that she wanted to move to the public sector. When she heard about Sigrid's new position, Charlotte envisioned her whipping into shape whole parkfuls of Columbusites with her relentless exercising.

Melanie Stevenson got a job as a telemarketer, and Charlotte thought her ability to hound people would be a real asset for the job. She continued her relationship with Barry Abrams, who opened an American primitive art gallery in the Short North section of Columbus once the Son of Heaven show closed. Charlotte eventually learned that the two of them had been together in Barry's Columbus Central office the night Phil was killed.

Lou became famous among her fellow Son of Heaven volunteers for her part in the necklace escapade and even gave a short lecture on the subject.

Charlotte quickly completed her articles about the neck-

lace and Stevenson's death. Although hers were not the first
stories about the necklace, no other writers were as knowledgeable or had her access to the people involved in the
case. Her stories sold very profitably and she celebrated
by buying an expensive necklace for herself. It was not
jade.

Printed in the United States
By Bookmasters